For imformation regarding permission please contact:
Golden Edition Publishing 108 N. Locust St. Suite 300 Denton, TX 76201
www.goldeneditionpublishing.com

Library of Congress Control Number: 2017952790
ISBN 978-0-9992361-1-6 (ebook)
ISBN 978-0-9992361-0-9 (paperback)
ISBN 978-0-9992361-3-0 (hardcover)
ISBN 978-0-9992361-2-3 (audio book)

Printed in the United States of America

CRW 10987654321, First Edition

What Kinda Name is Blart?
Chewing Problems

written by
Dominic Cosme

Illustrations by
Stephanie Will

Golden Edition
Publishing, Inc.
Denton, Texas USA

This book is written is a style that emphasizes the main character's (Blart) speech impediment. You will find sensational spellings and cacography throughout, they are purposeful and necessary to portray the spirit of the story. Younger readers may need assistance with understanding the use of these words.

Chapter 1

Crash, brrrr, ka-chunk ka-chunk. It had been going on all night. When would it stop? Only two days left in summer vacation and no one wants to wake up at... "Mom, what time is it?"... no answer. "**Mom**!!!"

She came running into the room, stubbing her toe on the doorjamb. "Ow!" she howled, hopping on one foot with her hair stuck up to one side. "What on earth are you doing up? It's too early. You need to go back to sleep, young man."

"I can't Mom. All night all I've heard is that." *Crash, brrrr, ka-chunk ka-chunk.* The sound came again, just like before. His mom moved toward the window to look outside. The moving trucks came around eight o'clock last night and were still in the neighbor's driveway.

"It sure seems weird to move into a new house in the middle of the night," she said, "and I haven't even seen the new neighbors yet."

It was weird all right, that they would move here at all. Great, Charlie moved away at the beginning of the summer, leaving me with the cruddiest vacation ever. Now we have night moving weirdos next door. Crud!

"Well, as long as you're up, how about pancakes for breakfast?" She headed off down the hall toward the kitchen. *Crash, brrrr, ka-chunk ka-chunk.*

"Arrrrghhhh!" Teddy pulled the pillow over his face. "And keep it down, young man. Your father is still trying to sleep."

Teddy jumped up and went straight to the closet. He had secretly been marking his height on the inside of the door frame. Being the smallest kid in class was hard. He had been eating all summer in hopes that he'd grow a little bigger, huge meals too. Putting his hand on top of his head, he turned around in anticipation. His hand still covered the mark he had made at the end of school. *Not an inch, not even a fraction of an inch.* Teddy sighed deeply. It seemed the only thing he was growing was a continual bellyache. He guessed the hope of growing six inches in two days was kind of dumb.

Teddy was always the smallest kid in class. He just turned nine, but everyone thought he was more like five or six. His mom would always tell him "greatness comes in small packages," like that was supposed to help him feel better, but it didn't. It also didn't help when he lost his front teeth at the age of six, and his adult teeth grew in with a big gap between them that made him talk funny. Add that to the lack of stature, and it was easy for people to mistake his age.

Again, he sighed. *I have Action Hero Crime Fighter pajamas and sheets*, he thought to himself. *If you know anything about kids, you know that five-year-olds aren't old enough to appreciate the sophistication of "Action Hero" crime fighting. They're still caught up in little ponies, cars, and choo-choos, **not** the stuff of nine-year-olds!*

He reluctantly got dressed to the clunking and banging sound coming from next door. As he was brushing his hair, or what his dad liked to call the mop on his head, he noticed it had gotten quiet. He looked outside from the living room window on his way toward the kitchen and noticed the trucks were starting to leave. *Weirdos*, he thought again. Then, out of the corner of his eye as the last truck pulled away, he saw it.

Sitting on the lawn and waiting to be brought in was the

Super Mondo Ultra Mega Action Hero Bed, the complete set, with action hero sides and attachable rocket fins. It was what he always wanted. He asked for one on his birthday, and instead, he got the pajama set and sheets. "Whoa, Mom! Guess what!" he called. "Guess what!" He headed toward the kitchen with instant excitement.

"Shhhh!" she called back. "Your dad is still sleeping."

"Not with all this noise," Dad commented, stepping into the living room. He grabbed Teddy up and tickled him, making him laugh. "Now, what's this I hear about pancakes?"

Chapter 2

Standing in front of the kitchen sink and looking at the house next door, Teddy's father kept moving back and forth, trying to get a better view. "The windows are still drawn shut. I can't see anything."

"Come back and sit down," Teddy's mom urged. "You are starting to look strange. If you keep shifting in the window like that, the neighbors might think you're spying."

"So what?" Teddy's dad commented as he sat down. "If you don't want people to get curious, don't move in the middle of the night. Do it during the day, like normal people."

"Maybe they moved at night to avoid curious people like you?" she mentioned, but as she said it, she got a funny feeling.

"Exactly my point, honey."

"Did you see the Super Mondo Ultra Mega Action Hero Bed? Huh, Dad? Did you?" Teddy interrupted, trying his best to hold back his excitement. "Did you?"

"Now, Teddy," his Dad said, "we have no idea where the new neighbors are from, and it still seems strange they moved in overnight. I don't want you going over there, even if you saw what looked like that bed you want. We haven't met them yet."

His dad looked at his mom for support. Teddy knew that look. His mom would jump on the same side as his dad.

"I'm sure we'll have a chance to meet them soon, Teddy. Your dad is right."

Bummer. They went straight for the gang-up. This has to be the worst summer ever. "They can't be that bad. They bought a bed like that for their kid," he said, hoping that they would suddenly change their minds. The look he got told him, *don't push your luck.*

"Well, can I at least go in the backyard and play?" he asked instead.

"Sure, I don't see why not." His dad said.

Stepping onto the back porch, Teddy made his way to an open area. He had gotten a super bouncy ball out of a vending machine at the grocery store and had been trying to bounce it higher and higher for the last week. He never seemed to get it any higher though. His arm was still a little sore from the hundreds of throws he had made, but the thrill was in the challenge of it. He liked challenges. His mom was always saying he had something to prove, because of his size. People always thought he looked younger than he actually was. When anyone gave him a challenge, he loved to see their reaction when he'd exceed their expectations.

Teddy tried his best to distract himself from his thoughts. Even as he bounced the ball, chased it down, and bounced it again, his mind kept wandering back to the bed. *Who did it belong to?* Teddy knew it had to be a boy, not a girl. *Girls don't like Action Heroes; everybody knows that. Besides, girls are gross. It has to be a boy!* He could already see them becoming good friends. The new kid must be into Action Heroes with a bed like that, so the chances were good. Teddy thought his mom would have been happy about someone his age moving in. Since Charlie left at the end of school, she kept saying he was just moping around.

Teddy kept bouncing the ball and daydreaming, when an odd bark came from behind the fence. He almost missed it at first, but the sound was so strange it snapped him out of his thoughts. Looking at the fence, Teddy noticed something moving on the other side.

"Grrraaarrk, Grrraaarrk!"

What kind of animal makes a noise like that, Teddy wondered. Suddenly, another strange sound emerged from behind the fence.

"HHHrrrggghhhh!"

Teddy squinted at the fence to get a better look. He could see movement on the other side between the slats. The size and shape told him it was probably a medium-sized dog. Plus, he could see the paws below the fence line running back and forth. Teddy listened for a while, trying to hear the odd bark again, but the dog had gone quiet. He really wasn't sure what the other sound was, so he shrugged it off and slammed the ball as hard as he could against the pavement.

"Grrraaarrk, Grrraaarrk."

The strange bark came again. Teddy looked at the fence again and noticed every time the ball went above the fence line, the strange bark would ring out. It was funny. The sound had a certain excitement behind it. Teddy could tell how badly the dog wanted to play with the ball. Laughing, Teddy bounced the ball again. He didn't pay attention to the angle of his throw. The ball ricocheted off the house and over the fence. The shadow between the slats suddenly raced off in the direction of the ball.

"Uh oh." Teddy watched the ball fall out of sight. He knew it was a goner as he approached the fence. That dog really wanted the ball. It was obvious. Teddy was still laughing to himself when he reached the fence line. *What a silly bark,* he thought. Looking up, Teddy tried to put his foot on the middle piece of wood all fences have. He was of the personal opinion fences were made like that so kids could climb them. His dad seemed to have another opinion, though, because he was always yelling at Teddy to get down. Unfortunately, he still couldn't reach it without stepping on something first.

"Couldn't I have at least grown an inch? I guess I'll have to go the hard way then," Teddy mumbled to himself, turning toward the opposite side of the yard.

Their house had a small wall that hid the air conditioning unit, and it was the only place he could get onto the fence. Teddy studied his path. He'd have to shimmy across one side, to the back, across that, then back up toward the house on the other side. He wouldn't have had to go so far a few years ago; but when his previous neighbor, Charlie, lived there, his dad built a shed that blocked the back half of their yard. The only way to see where the ball went was to make the complete circuit. Timing was everything. If his parents saw him on the fence it was over; he'd never get a glimpse of the other side. Teddy needed to hurry. Plus, who knows what would happen to that ball if the dog got a hold of it?

"Here goes nothing," he said as he hiked himself on the wall. Looking toward the back of his house, he checked to see what he might find in the windows. No sight of Mom and Dad. That was good. He could make this quick. Stepping off the ledge and onto the fence, he immediately slipped.

Strike one!, Teddy thought to himself, as he climbed back onto the wall. "Ok," he said out loud, "maybe not that quick." He looked around the yard to validate he was still clear, hopped back onto the fence, and began to shimmy across. When he rounded the last corner by the shed, he paused long enough to look back and make sure no one was watching. All of a sudden, the oddest sounds started from the other side of the fence.

Drat! The shed was still in the way! Hurrying as fast as he could, he managed to get his head clear of the shed in time to see the wildest sight he might have ever witnessed. On the opposite side of the fence was a strange-looking kid and a dog with a backward tail.

Chapter 3

"Huh?" the sound escaped him before he even realized it.

"Grrraaarrk!" The dog headed toward the fence wagging its tail, or what you might consider the act of wagging its tail. Really, it was just flopping over in odd ways back and forth. In fact, it looked like it had been pulled off and reattached at an awkward angle, a little too much to one side. It looked backward too. The dog grabbed a bone with his mouth and started running back and forth below the fence. *Well, if he has a bone, maybe my ball is still safe,* Teddy thought.

"Whatt rrrrr you doooing?"

Teddy looked up because it sounded like a question. That's when he noticed there was a bone in the kids mouth too.

"Why are you chewing on a bone?" Teddy asked.

"I neeeded ssomethinggg tooo bite onn."

"Oh, OK," Teddy responded, "that makes sense." Looking below him, Teddy saw it was clear and proceeded to hop over. "Hey, I lost my ball when it bounced over the fence. Have you seen it?"

"It'ss overr therrre," the new kid pointed. Teddy looked across the yard and spotted it.

"You talk pretty funny," Teddy commented. "You have an accent. That's what my mom calls it anyway. Where are you from? New York? I bet it's New York. There are a lot of accents

there. I've never been, but I met a kid at camp, and he talked kind of funny. Not like you, kinda different and a little faster. Anyway, he was from New York."

The kid gave him a strange look and changed the subject. "Dooo you havvvve aaa name?"

"Oh, sorry, I guess I should have told you my name first. I'm Theodore Michael Chamberlain Millstone III, but everyone calls me Teddy. "Pleased to meet you. I'm your neighbor"

"I knooow thattt. You jummmped the fennccce."

"Well, I guess I didn't stop to think about you knowing I was from next door because I jumped the fence. Anyway, you must be smart to know that. What's your name?"

"Bblllaaaaarrrrt"

Teddy couldn't quite make it out but didn't want to be rude and ask again. "That sounds a little hard to pronounce, and I don't want to get it wrong. How about I just shorten it to Blart?"

Blart gave Teddy a strange look. He could only assume what Teddy referred to as an accent interfered with his hearing. Blart was about to inform him that was what he said but figured it might come across as insulting. Besides, Teddy got it right anyway. Deciding not to point it out, Blart shrugged instead. He put the bone back in his mouth and stood up clumsily, almost falling over in the process.

"Gosh, you're big. Maybe that's why you stood up funny," Teddy analyzed, watching Blart stumble. "My mom says big people have trouble with balance, but not me. I have great balance because I am so close to the ground." As Blart rose to his full height, Teddy saw he had misjudged. "You're huge!" Teddy exclaimed. Blart was clearly a head and a half taller than Teddy.

"I'mm onlyy nnine."

"Really! You're only nine?" Teddy responded, looking up, way up, at the bone hanging out of Blart's mouth. "I'm nine too. Everyone thinks I'm younger, because of my size, but I'm nine. I'll be in fourth grade this year." Teddy suddenly got excited. "Hey, you're nine! That means we are going to be in the same class."

Moving across the yard and retrieving his ball, Teddy looked back. The dog was wagging that silly tail so hard with excitement, it looked like it might just fall off. "What's your dog's name?" Teddy asked.

"Paatcchhhess," said Blart.

"Patches," Teddy repeated, laughing a little. It fit, especially when you looked at that tail. Patches took off at the sound of his name, running in circles and barking his odd bark. Teddy laughed again at the silly sight of a dog running in circles, barking at a kid with a bone in his mouth. That's when Teddy noticed the big scar across Blart's head. "Wow, were you in an accident?" Teddy blurted without thinking, trying to get a better look. Teddy noticed it wasn't one but two scars side-by-side, which made it look big from a distance. As Teddy looked closer, he started to notice more and more scars. They were practically everywhere, not just on his head, but across his arms and legs too.

"I'mm acccidennnnt-prrrone," Blart responded.

Accident-prone for sure, Teddy thought, *with that many scars*. His mom used the same phrase when she would talk about his cousin. The one who came to stay the night, who fell on the stairs, who fell out of bed, who fell off the chair, who fell just walking down the hall. Teddy thought he just had a problem with gravity but his mom called him "accident-prone."

"My cousin has that," Teddy said. "Don't worry. Stick with me, and I'll help you get over that." Looking more closely at the scars, Teddy noticed an odd coloring. It looked as if Blart's skin was slightly green.

"Are you on some kind of medicine? I don't mean to ask," Teddy asked, "but I noticed you look kinda green. My dad had to take this medicine once that turned him completely orange. He was like that for a month. I also had a teacher who had to take something that turned her yellow."

Blart just looked at Teddy and put the bone back into his mouth. He really didn't know how to respond. Teddy hadn't noticed how strange it was at first, but that's when the weirdness of the whole situation hit him.

"Do you have a biting problem?" Teddy asked. "Is that why you keep chewing on that bone? My cousin has a biting problem too. He's only three, but he has bitten everybody at his preschool. My aunt says it's because he's teething, but I think it's just cause he likes to bite." Teddy looked at the bone in Blart's mouth. "Well, we can't bring a bone to school, so we gotta get you over that biting problem. I think I can help, so don't worry. I've gotta go now, because my mom said I shouldn't be over here yet. If anyone asks, I was just over here getting my ball, OK?" Teddy started toward the fence. "I'll come back later and we can start working on that biting problem for you." He looked around but saw no way to get on the fence. "Umm, by the way, do you think I can get a boost?"

Chapter 4

Looking into the backyard, Ally gasped. "Tom, come here!" Tom came running into the den. Ally was pacing back and forth in front of the window. "Oh dear," she was saying, shaking her head.

"What is it, Ally?"

"Look," she replied, pointing. Tom followed her finger and peered out the window. There, in the backyard, was a little boy.

"I think he hopped the fence," said Ally. "Oh dear, what are we going to do?"

Tom looked at Ally again. "Well now, let's not overreact." Tom was a little worried himself, though he wouldn't admit it. Ally looked at Tom, clearly worried, then out the window again. She was mumbling something under her breath.

It wouldn't have mattered if she uttered it clearly, because Tom was watching the scene unfold outside. He really hoped Bartholomew would be accepted here and make new friends. Having a little boy next door to play with might be good for him. The thing was, Bartholomew was a very special child. He was the sweetest child really, but because of his size, awkwardness, and condition, he never really fit in.

Gazing out the window, Tom watched the boys interact. Patches was clearly excited, running around awkwardly, his tail looking like it was about to come off again. Tom started thinking back to where it began. It had all started with Patches. Tom thought about the day Patches ran off in the park. Bartholomew was about two, and the family had planned to go to the city park for a day of fun. Shortly after arriving, though, Patches managed to disappear. They searched for him for over an hour, walking the entire park three times. Ally finally found him. He was completely covered in mud and dirt, so it was obvious he had gotten into something. You couldn't even see his tufts of fur, which was why they had named him Patches to begin with. He was a Chinese Crested breed. That meant he was bald, except for a few patches of hair that stuck up around his face and covered his paws. Little did they know how appropriate the name would eventually become.

The same night, as Ally and Tom cleaned Patches, they started noticing an odd color around his eyes and mouth. They decided they would need to take Patches to the vet in the morning and have him checked, just in case. Later that night, Bartholomew was playing with Patches, as they often did, chasing each other through the house. Bartholomew let out a loud unexpected cry, and Ally rushed to see what had happened. Patches had nipped Bartholomew, and he was holding his hand crying. It was so unlike Patches to do anything like that. They scolded Patches, put him into his kennel, and proceeded to clean Bartholomew's hand. It wasn't bad, just a small scratch at the top of his finger on his left hand. Tom remembered Ally gently washing and bandaging it up for him. She was made to be a mother. Bartholomew was their first child, and she was very close to delivering their second around the time this happened.

The next day came, and with it, their lives would never be the same. Bartholomew was feeling bad and had an odd color around his eyes and mouth like Patches did the night before. They quickly checked on Patches, who seemed to be getting worse. Wasting no time, they packed up the car and headed out. They dropped Patches off into the vet's care and rushed to the doctor for Bartholomew. Immediately upon seeing him, the doctor put Bartholomew in the hospital.

Ally had their second child while their son was in the hospital, a little girl named Sarah. In fact, they had been concerned that they may never get Bartholomew out. It took some thorough tests and long durations of time to finally discover what ailed Bartholomew and Patches. A new bacteria was actually found by the vet taking care of Patches. It seemed Patches was exposed, and when he bit Bartholomew, he exposed him as well. The doctors eventually came up with a cure. They would no longer be contagious, but their exposure to the bacteria would have other effects that would remain.

Bartholomew had started growing by leaps and bounds. The doctors could only contribute it to his condition. His color never returned, and he tended to chew on things when he got nervous. Again, the doctors could only contribute this to his condition. It was a learning experience for the whole family, and whenever Bartholomew displayed a new behavior or physical quality, the doctors would default to his condition. Zombifinitis.

"Tom...**Tom!**"

That brought Tom back from his thought to the present. "Sorry, Ally. I was just thinking back...you know."

Ally did know. Things had changed so much since then. "I was just thinking we should probably go over and introduce ourselves to the neighbors. I'd like Blart to get to know the boy next door before he goes to school. It might help calm his nerves on the first day."

Tom looked at the little boy. "Well, he doesn't seem to

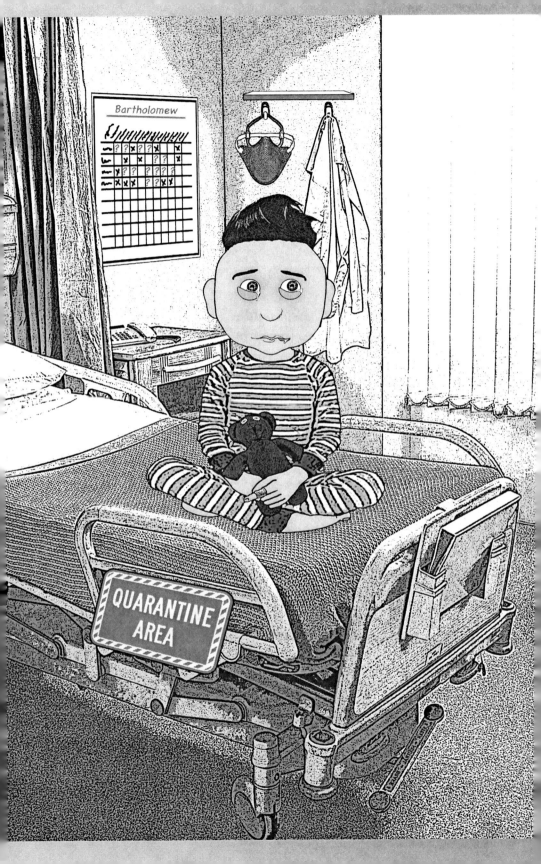

react like the other kids have. I guess that's a good start. I don't think he looks old enough to be in school with him though. We'll just have to see."

They watched their son help the boy back over the fence. Blart turned and awkwardly hurried, stumbling toward the house. Opening the door, he smiled as all excited kids do. "Gueesss whatt! I mettt the neighhborr kiddd. He'sss innn fourrrth graaade!" he exclaimed excitedly.

"Well, that's perfect! You'll already know someone in your class!" Ally couldn't help but be excited for him. "Tell you what. Why don't we see if... what's his name?"

"Tedddyyy," Blart responded.

"Teddy, oh what a cute name! Well, as I was saying," Ally continued, "we were just talking about introducing ourselves to the neighbors. Why don't we see if Teddy can show you around a little? Your dad and I can continue to get the house in order. What do you think?"

"I'd liiike thaaat." Blart flashed a big grin.

Tom couldn't help it. He loved seeing his children happy, and the grin on Bartholomew's face was priceless. Moving here was his gift to Ally and the kids. Living in the city had been hard after Bartholomew came home from the hospital. The noise and continual humdrum was not good for his condition, and Ally was having a hard time watching the effects on her son. Moving to a less active area was the only thing Tom could think of to help, so he found this house. When he first showed it to Ally, she almost started crying. This really confused him until she said it was perfect; then he realized that they were tears of joy. That was all it took, and Tom bought the house.

"I guess we should get ready to meet the neighbors then," he commented to Ally. As she turned toward him, he saw a slight nervousness in her eyes. "Don't worry. This will be great," he whispered to her, as he watched Blart head off down the hall.

Chapter 5

Back over the fence, Teddy looked around the yard. No sign of Mom and Dad. That was good. He felt a little guilty, but it really wasn't his fault the ball went into the neighbor's yard. It was an accident. He was just getting his ball back, that's all.

It had been a huge risk since it was Saturday. His dad was off from his typical day job, so that meant beating four eyes, instead of two like during the week. His mom was predictable. She tended to stay in the house; but his Dad, he was always popping up outside doing some kind of crazy chore and mumbling about always working. Sometimes he would trap Teddy into working with him. Character building, he would call it; but really, it was just a way to suck the fun out of the day and share the misery. That was what Teddy thought, anyway. Getting caught up in work, especially the last weekend before school started, was definitely not fun.

In fact, shortly after Teddy learned to read, his Dad suckered him into work by saying it would be fun. Later that night, Teddy showed up to the dinner table with a dictionary and proceeded to read the definition of fun. He struggled a little with the bigger words, but he really wanted his Dad to know, so he wouldn't get confused in the future. His mom chuckled a little while he read, but Dad fell out of his chair with laughter. "Hearing you read that," his Dad hooted, "now that was fun!"

Teddy made it into the house without anyone being the

wiser. It seemed his Dad was aiming for a lazy weekend of watching sports. He liked to turn on the channel that shows a dozen sports at the same time. Then he'd turn on the picture-in-picture setting with the other sports channel that showed another eight sports. That's right, a total of twenty sports channels all together. *Dad never watches the "good" ones though,* Teddy thought. *He likes the odd ones like the Worldwide Curling Channel, Lawn Bowling Network, Caber Tossing Extreme, Ga-ga Ball TV, Underwater Hockey Vision, and Toe Wrestling HD. Never the good ones! Maybe he does it just to annoy Mom; it does tend to work quickly. She'll ask him when he plans to clean the garage or mow the lawn. He'll roll his eyes and start mumbling about work again. It's just a vicious cycle.*

"Where's Mom?" Teddy asked.

"Getting ready, which leaves me just enough time to catch up on my sports," he answered.

Teddy walked off down the hall toward his room. *Whew! None the wiser,* he thought as he reached the computer desk. Now it was time to get busy. He had a lot of work to do to get Blart ready for school and over the biting problem. Biting tended to get you into big trouble; and Teddy wasn't sure, but he figured it would get you into even bigger trouble in the fourth grade.

Sitting at his desk, he turned on the computer and started his research. It turned out there were quite a few methods on how to stop biting. There were a couple of methods he chose to throw out immediately, as they seemed a little strange, but there were still many suggestions left. After he had gathered a big enough list of methods, he sat back and studied the options, feeling good about helping Blart. He knew exactly what he would do. *I'll go down the list and try each option*, Teddy thought to himself with confidence. His dad often said, "planning was the most important step," so Teddy took extra time to make sure he developed a good plan. The only thing left to do now was gather his materials. He was pretty sure he could find what was needed, if he just looked hard enough.

He went to the closet and found his backpack from last year tucked away on a shelf. *OK, step one accomplished.* Teddy was only on the first step, and already his plan was going perfectly. Picking up the backpack, he slung it over his shoulder, and smiled to himself as he left the room. Heading down the hall to find the rest of the materials he was looking for, he couldn't help but feel confident in his planning abilities.

After about fifteen uneventful minutes of gathering supplies, a voice sounded over his shoulder, stopping him square in his tracks. *Uh-oh*, he had forgotten about Mom. She must have been in stealth mode because he never even heard her approach.

"What are you up to, young man? Why on earth would you be going through all the kitchen drawers, and what are you doing with that old backpack? You know good and well I bought a new one this year. I have already filled it with your school supplies, so you're all set for Monday," she said while her eyes narrowed.

Teddy tried to distract her. "Yeah, I know. You worked so hard on it, I really wanted to say thank you, Mom." Teddy used his sweetest voice, trying to butter her up.

She looked at him, like all moms, with super suspicion. Not really at him so much as through him, straight to the backpack on his shoulder. She knew something was going on. The flattery didn't seem to be working, and he had nothing else to distract her with.

*Oh, great. This was not... I repeat, **not**... part of my plan. What else can I do?* Teddy thought to himself. Something from the educational channels suddenly flashed through his mind. It was crazy, but he figured he would try it anyway, so he held his breath and remained perfectly still. If he didn't move, she might not see him.

He knew it was ridiculous since she wasn't a T-Rex; and besides, who really knew if that worked anyway? Teddy figured it was a good bet if you ever encountered a dinosaur, of any kind, remaining still might not be the best option. He really didn't know much about dinosaurs; and in fact, he had never met anyone who had seen a dinosaur. Probably because anyone who might have seen one liked to stay still at the wrong time, he reasoned.

Teddy was amazed that it actually worked. His mom just shook her head and asked, "What's your father doing?" He decided to file his method away for later, just in case he had to use his sudden stillness on his mom again.

"Catching up on sports! He seems to think he might get a long day of watching TV."

Teddy stretched the truth a little with the last part of the comment, but it worked. His mom was already heading toward the den, totally focused on assigning Dad a new project. "Stay still, point to Dad." Teddy whispered quietly to himself.

That was too close! Now Teddy would have to hurry and get the last few items he needed before the plan went entirely astray. He also needed to figure out how to avoid his dad, or he might end up getting drafted into working. It was too important to take that risk. He needed to make sure Blart was over his problem before Monday. Heading toward the garage to find the last few items, a thought occurred to Teddy.

How am I going to get permission to go over to the neighbors' house? His mom and dad had made it clear they didn't want him to go over there until they were able to meet the neighbors first. *That was it!* All Teddy had to do was figure out how to get them together. Time was wasting, so he picked up his pace and double-timed it to the garage.

Chapter 6

All packed up with the tools he needed, Teddy was at a loss on how he could set up a meeting between his parents and the neighbors. There was no way to get them together, he knew, because had been pondering it for about thirty minutes. Resting his head upon his desk and feeling pressured, Teddy mumbled to himself, "think, think, think." Time was not on his side, and this had put him behind.

The doorbell rang, and Teddy was pulled from his thoughts for a minute. He looked outside but couldn't see anything. *Who was it?* Moving out of his room and toward the front door, he saw his mom standing with the door open, talking to someone. Stepping closer, he managed a glimpse outside. In the doorway were a man and woman whom he didn't recognize.

"Well, it is certainly nice to meet you," his mom was saying. "We noticed the trucks arrive last night."

It was the neighbors! This might just work in his favor. He had been sweating how to get them together, and here they were. Teddy continued to watch from the side of the room, trying not to get noticed.

The man spoke. "Sorry about the noise, unfortunately we got delayed and the movers were going to charge us for another day if we didn't get everything off the trucks. I hope we didn't disturb you too much."

"Of course not," his mom said to be polite.

They continued their conversation, and Teddy wondered how he could turn this into an advantage. The neighbors meeting his mom like this knocked out his first problem, and he didn't even have to do anything. Teddy thought this might be a good thing and could possibly turn out in his favor somehow. He decided to let it unfold on it's own and just see where it went. He had promised Blart he would be back to help, and this had been a roadblock.

"Before we go," the woman said, "I was just wondering if you happen to have a little boy."

"Yes. Teddy. Why?"

"We just noticed him climb over the fence earlier."

Uh-oh, Teddy thought. *Nope... this is definitely not a good thing.*

"Bartholomew, our son, is very excited about meeting your son," she continued. "It is all he's been talking about this morning. We hope they have a chance to become better friends before school starts. He mentioned Teddy was going into the fourth grade. That's the same grade as Bartholomew. I would really appreciate it if your son could show him around a little. The move has been tough on him, and he has been extremely nervous about meeting new friends. Anyway, I just wanted to let you know he's free for the day if your son wants to come over and play."

Teddy's mom flashed a tight-lipped smile, he knew well. "OK, I'll let Teddy know. Maybe after lunch... we'll see."

Teddy started backing out of the room and managed to bump into a table. His mom looked his direction as she closed the door. "Well?" she asked, tapping her foot.

He decided to play dumb, trying to distract her. "Who was that?"

"Theodore?"

She had used his real name. That was never good. It was mixed with the tone of a question, and Teddy knew that meant it was even worse. Her eyebrow raised and Teddy cracked.

"I'm sorry, Mom. It wasn't my fault. It was an accident. I promise. The ball bounced over the fence and they have a dog. I was worried the dog would eat it or something, so I had to jump the fence to get the ball back. Honest."

Teddy's mom looked at him, still tapping her foot. Even though it was the truth, she wasn't buying it. "If it wasn't for the fact that their son is going to be in school with you and doesn't know anyone here, you'd be in big trouble right now. We will discuss this later, so don't think you got away with it. I intend to collect through chores."

Teddy's shoulders sank. "I know," he mumbled under his breath. His mom liked to discipline through chores. When he was five, he was always getting into trouble. His mom gave him every chore she could possibly think of. "You could tell Teddy's behavior by the condition of the house," his dad would say laughingly. During that time, Teddy was suspicious his mom might have made up a few chores, just to prove a point.

"All right, young man. It's time for lunch. Let's go make some sandwiches, and we can talk to your father about this afternoon." She headed toward the kitchen with Teddy in tow.

Chapter 7

Knocking on the door, Teddy waited and thought more about his plan. He knew he had some good ideas. The door opened a crack, and a little girl looked out at Teddy. "Are you that kid from next door?" she asked, without giving Teddy time to answer. "You don't look like you're in fourth grade. You probably just said that because you can't count. You look too small to be old enough to be in the fourth grade. Don't you know you have to be nine?"

Teddy just looked and blinked, taken aback. "What?" he finally managed to utter.

"Oh no, it must be worse than I thought if that confused you." She opened the door wider. "Maybe you're just a very big four-year-old. That would make sense. That would explain why you don't know school ages yet."

"I know school ages!" Teddy exclaimed. "I should. I've been there for four years. Kindergarten, first, second, and third grade. I'm small for my age." He really hated having to explain his size to people. Plus, he could tell she was younger than him despite being the same size. Sarah's eyes narrowed with suspicion. Teddy thought of a good quip, "I would tell you to ask me a fourth grade question, but you wouldn't know any, so it doesn't matter. Is Blart here?"

"See, that proves it. You can't even pronounce his name. What kind of name is Blart? Anyone in fourth grade wouldn't talk like a baby." Doing nothing but confusing Teddy, she

turned around and yelled, "**Bart**! There is an oversized toddler here to see you."

Bart! That was his name, not Blart. He was about to comment on how it was just a misunderstanding, when her full statement sank in. "Hey!" Teddy exclaimed, "I am not a toddler! I'm nine and have been for months!"

"Whatever," she said as she ran off.

Teddy put his hand on his head. *Girls are weird*, he thought. He never understood them and was of the opinion they never really understood themselves. Half of the girls he knew would say boys are stinky and gross, but every day at recess they would chase them, catch them, and try to kiss them. When Teddy pointed this out, they chased him, but he got punched not kissed. *Girls equate to weirdly weird*, he thought to himself.

"Hi. I'm sorry about that," a woman said as she reached the doorway. "I see you got a chance to meet Blart's sister, Sarah. I'm Ally." She opened the door all the way. "Won't you come in?" she invited. "I have to say, Blart is certainly excited to have a neighbor in his class at school, and we are too. Moving to a new place can be hard, and it would be nice if Blart had someone to help show him around. Thanks for coming over."

"I don't mind at all!" Teddy responded, not hiding his enthusiasm or confusion.

When he first heard Bart's name, he didn't quite catch it, so he had shortened it to what he heard, Blart. The kid didn't correct him, so he figured he had gotten it right. Sarah had just gone through the trouble of making a point that his name was Bart; but he could swear, he had just heard Ally call him Blart. He was definitely confused. "I've got a question though, is his name Blart or Bart? I heard Sarah call him Bart."

Teddy really didn't want to call him by the wrong name.

"Well, that depends on who you meet first," she said with a smile. Teddy was now utterly confused. "I think Blart is in his room trying to set some things up. Follow me. I'll show you where it is."

Teddy looked around as they walked through the house. Everything had changed. It looked like Charlie had never even lived there. The walls had been painted and the kitchen had been updated with new appliances. There was a new extra wide fridge, the one with the fancy ice water dispenser. *Six different ice settings and four temperature modes, so you don't hurt your teeth or get brain freeze,* Teddy remembered from the commercials.

He followed Ally down the hall toward the back room, Charlie's old room. Teddy started to get a guilty feeling deep inside. He was still excited to get to know Blart, but he suddenly missed Charlie a whole lot. He had known things would change in both their lives after the move, and that was all right. It was the journey that made you, and they were on separate journeys right now. He thought about it for a second and figured; *Charlie wouldn't mind if a kid with the coolest bed in town moved into his old room. At least it wasn't Blart's sister, Sarah.*

Chapter 8

"Blart, honey. You have someone here to see you," Ally announced.

Blart looked up and saw Teddy in the doorway. "Ccommme onn innn," he invited. Blart was crouched on the floor hunkered over a side slat of his bed. He was trying to finish piecing it together.

"Whoa! It's even cooler in real life!" Teddy walked over and bent down next to Blart. He began running a hand slowly down the edge of the bed, looking at the perfect side molding. The way the paint glossed upon the frame was unreal. "I love Action Hero Crime Fighters!" Teddy exclaimed. "I have all of their videos and action figures. I even asked for this exact bed for my birthday, but I got the sheet and pajama set instead. Can I help you set up the fins?" Teddy asked.

Blart smiled a wonky grin. "Of courssse," he said, handing Teddy a screwdriver and picking up a fin.

"Well, I can see you two have a few things in common," Ally said. "I'll be in the living room unpacking if you guys need anything. Have fun." She walked off, heading down the hall. "Oh yeah, I have snacks if you get hungry. Just let me know," she called back.

"Wow. Your mom is nice," Teddy commented as he watched her leave, "but your sister is kind of weird." Blart laughed.

Looking around the room, Teddy noticed they were

definitely into the same things. There was the Action Hero Crime Fighter connection, of course, but it didn't stop there. He had Mega Robot Morpher posters, Air Strike Command Force action planes, and Creato-Destructo interlocking construction blocks. He even had a Desert Alien Space Traveler attack ship with RC hovering capabilities. Everyone knew that the attack ship with hovering capabilities was a limited collector's edition. Only 2000 were made, and each one came with certificates of authentication. They had sequential numbers matching the production off the factory line, and they were rarer than rare. In fact, this was the first one Teddy had ever seen that wasn't an image on a computer. "No way! Where did you get one of those?"

"Whenn I wasss in the hossspitalll," Blart responded.

That took Teddy aback for a moment. "Oh, you were in the hospital?" Teddy wondered why but knew it was wrong to ask. Blart looked like he had been in an accident, but he never mentioned anything when Teddy asked before, so he decided he shouldn't pry. "Well, I'm glad you're out, and you seem fine to me, so that's good. What model number is your attack ship?" Teddy asked knowing full well the fact that he had an attack ship at all was enough. It really didn't matter if it was the first or the last.

"Nummmberr fourrr," Blart said. He stood up clumsily and headed across the room. Retrieving the card sitting next to the attack ship on his bookshelf, he handed it to Teddy.

Looking at the card, Teddy's eyes almost popped out of his head. Right there on the front was an imprint, 0004/2000. That meant this was the fourth one off the production line. The fourth one they ever made! "Holy-moly, you got number four!" he exclaimed with all the excitement he could muster, which really wasn't hard at all. Teddy grinned from ear to ear.

He couldn't help but feel this was the beginning of a great friendship. They were the same age and liked the same things too, which were two of the most important things to build a good friendship.

Teddy looked around some more and spotted a computer on the desk. "Is that the SuperXP-400LE Trista gaming computer?" he asked, but really didn't need to. He knew exactly what it was from the shape of the monitor. "I have the standard model. It's about three years old. I've been asking to upgrade, but my parents keep telling me I have to wait. My dad upgraded the memory for me though, so it is about one level under yours. That's cool. We can play games together when we can't hang out. I mostly stick to the racing games right now because they are easy to play alone, but I have a feeling that will be changing real soon."

Blart smiled a wonky grin and nodded, "Rrreall soooon!" They continued to finish the rocket fin attachments on the bed and talked about everything they could think of. They were a lot alike, and it felt good to have a new friend with so much in common.

"Hey," Teddy commented, "Charlie and I had a phone system we made with a string and cups when he lived here. My mom said I couldn't have a real phone until my age was in the double digits. According to that logic, I could be 99 before I get one. Charlie and I couldn't wait that long; so instead, we decided to go "old school". I don't know what that means, but it's what my dad kept calling it. Anyway, we never took down the string, and you're in the same room." He jumped up and headed to the window. Looking near the top, he spotted the string still hanging in the corner of the frame. It had been rolled up into a small ball, but it was still there. "We're in business," he commented over his shoulder. "It's still here."

Teddy almost couldn't believe it. He figured someone would have at least cut it by now, but there it was, tucked away and safe.

"Glaaad I didnnn't cuttt ittt. Ittt loooked immporrrtannt." Blart stumbled toward the window, reached up over Teddy, and pulled on the ball of string. It unraveled to floor with a good amount of length to it, but Teddy didn't notice. He was looking at Blart's arms as Blart was pulling on the string. There were more scars underneath he hadn't noticed before, and some looked like they had been real deep. *Man, that had to have been some accident*, Teddy thought. Blart noticed the look on Teddy's face and lowered his arms slowly. He backed away a little, trying to conceal the scars.

"What happened to you?" Teddy asked with deep concern, moving forward to get a better view. He could tell it must have been something drastic, almost life changing. Looking up at Blart, he could almost see a trace of anguish on his new friend's face. "It's OK if you don't want to talk about it, but if you do, I'm real good at keeping secrets. You don't know that about me yet, but you will. I promise. Friends need to have each other's back, and I will always have yours. That's the first rule in my book of friendship." Teddy smiled.

Blart relaxed a little and flashed a slight wonky grin. Teddy couldn't help but smile back. Blart looked at Teddy and pondered the dilemma. The truth of it wasn't that he didn't want to tell Teddy about his situation. It was more the fact there was so little known about his condition. Most people were terrified of it, quite frankly, and were continually misinformed about the real aspects of Zombifinitis. When the community he lived in before found out about his condition, they treated him like a monster. That was one of the top reasons they moved in the first place. His parents were adamant about giving him a normal life. Blart really didn't understand why people saw his condition as bad. He wasn't even contagious. "Some people are just narrow minded," his dad would explain when he asked. Blart knew he couldn't keep his condition a secret for long if they were going to be friends. Things always happened, and Teddy was bound to see some things he would continue to question if left in the dark. Something had to be done, or their friendship might be brief.

"Come onnn, let'sss gettt snacksss." Blart hoped his parents might be able to help. He felt like if Teddy could keep a secret, maybe it was worth a shot. If his parents wanted him to be normal and fit in, it would be helpful to have someone who knew about his condition. He would at least have someone who could help him if something happened at school. With Blart's track record of being accident-prone, something was bound to happen. Probably sooner than later.

Chapter 9

Making their way toward the kitchen, the pair looked like they had been friends their whole lives, talking with excitement about Blart's new room. Ally was amazed. They seemed to have so much in common, it was as if they were made to be friends. Blart was happy and excited. It was obvious. She could tell. But there was also a slight worry behind his eyes that Ally recognized.

"Teddy, do you like cookies?" Ally asked with a smile. She knew all kids Teddy's age liked cookies. It was a trick question.

"Doesn't everybody?" Teddy smiled.

Ally laughed and opened the fridge. "Well, I hope you like milk with your cookies." She grabbed the carton out of the fridge and filled two glasses, handing one to Blart and one to Teddy. She then pulled a jar from the top shelf of the pantry, placed the cookies on a plate, and headed toward the table.

Ally watched the boys dip and eat their cookies thinking hard on her next move. She really wished Tom was here, but he had gone to the hardware store for a few items. Ally knew Blart was different, and the more time someone spent with him, more differences would be seen and questioned. She knew this worried him, since previous outcomes had not gone well, and she could see the nervousness when he ate his cookies.

"Man, you must really like to savor your cookies,"

Teddy commented, watching Blart. He had been dipping and nibbling at them in small rapid bites. "I never thought of taking so many bites at one cookie. Seems like it might be the best way to enjoy it though. If you take more bites, it lasts longer. I guess you probably feel like you get more in the end." Teddy looked at his cookie, took a dip in the milk then proceeded to nibble on it like Blart.

Ally watched the transaction. Blart got more nervous, and started nibbling faster, like his teeth were chattering. "Clackety clack clack".

Teddy looked up. "Maybe the milk is too cold. Is that why your teeth keep chattering like that?" He looked at the milk, but Blart hadn't drunk any of it. He was just using it to dip the cookies. Well, that didn't any make sense. "Ohhh, maybe it's cold in here then." But Teddy didn't feel cold. In fact, it was hot and the end of summer, so that didn't make any sense either.

Blart looked at his mom while he took rapid bites from the cookie. "Teddy," Ally said, knowing that she had to do something, "Bartholomew is extremely glad that you came over. You two seem to have a lot in common."

Bartholomew, that was his name! That's why Sarah called him Bart. He filed it away. It was always good to know someone's full name.

Ally took another cookie trying to process her next thought. "He is unique though, and sometimes that's hard to overlook for people," she said.

"Well, he's the tallest fourth grader I've ever met. That makes him unique in my book. It's OK with me though." Teddy hopped down from his chair and rose to his full height. "See, I'm uniquely opposite," he said with a grin.

Ally looked at him and smiled. "It's a little more

than just his size or height. I want you to understand that Blart has a condition that is extremely rare."

"Is that why he was in the hospital?" Teddy blurted without thinking.

"Did Blart tell you about the hospital?" Ally asked, taken aback. She looked at Blart with a raised eyebrow, but he just continued to gnaw at the cookies getting more nervous.

"No. He just mentioned he got his Desert Alien Space Travelers Attack Ship while in the hospital. It didn't seem like he wanted to talk about it though, so I didn't ask much. I thought he was in an accident, because of the scars." He looked toward Blart and got a guilty feeling talking about it now. Blart obviously hadn't wanted to say anything and didn't while they were talking before.

Ally caught the look between them and placed a hand on Blart's shoulder. "I think Blart would feel better if you knew, but he's a little worried about it," she said.

Teddy didn't know what to think. He looked back and forth between Blart and Ally, trying to imagine what it could be. He wasn't quite sure, but his mind was racing. He thought about his uncle who had had emergency surgery because of appendicitis. His scar was pretty big and on his side, but Blart's scars were all over. If you looked close enough, you could see he had scars on top of scars.

He thought about his accident-prone cousin, the one falling everywhere, the one that was always running into walls or doorjambs. He could get paper cuts from just turning book pages. Although he was clumsy and had a few scars, his were nothing like Blart's. Mostly, his cousin just lived with a lot of bruises and an outrageous collection of ice packs. Teddy was so confused at this point. It was obvious, plain as day from the expression on his face. He was also so deep in thought he never noticed Sarah sat down at the table.

"Why are you making that face?" Sarah asked. "It's milk and cookies. You dunk the cookie and you eat it. This is what happens when an overgrown toddler tries to act nine. The confusion is obvious."

"What..." Teddy said, snapping out of his thoughts, "I...um...no. What?"

Sarah shook her head, "Oh man, this is bad. Worse than I thought. I guess I have to teach you. What kind of giant four-year-old doesn't know how to dunk cookies?"

Teddy put a hand on his forehead and slid it down to his chin, trying to wipe away the frustration building up inside. He had just met Sarah, and she already had a way of getting under his skin. It was unnatural. "I keep telling you, I am nine. I'm just small for my age."

"Yeah, whatever," Sarah responded.

Ally looked across the table. "Sarah!"

"What? I just call it as I see it, that's all."

"Teddy is our guest, and you are being rude!" Ally scolded.

"Sorry," Sarah mumbled, with a look behind her eyes that said otherwise. She took a cookie, held it outstretched in her hand, and made a wide, obvious arch toward the glass of milk. She dunked it several times, leaned over her glass and stared directly at Teddy as she slowly took a bite. The look in her eyes said it all.

Teddy shook his head. He decided to let it go and turned to look back at Ally, "So what happened? Why is Blart so worried?" he asked.

"**Bart** is always worried. It's part of the Zombifinitifitis, I mean the Zombifintinitus... Oh whatever! I can never say it!" Sarah blurted, still managing to emphasize the name, Bart, at the beginning of her statement.

"Sarah! We were getting to that!" Ally scolded.

"Zombifi-what?" Teddy blurted, looking toward his newest friend. He could see a deep concern and worry behind that wonky smile. Blart looked toward his sister, then back at Teddy, and finally settled his gaze on the cookies on his plate. The confusion was mounting in Teddy.

"The medical term is Zombifinitis," Ally said, giving Sarah another stern look before turning back to Teddy. "Zombifinitis is what doctors who studied the condition labeled it, anyway."

Teddy looked at Ally, not sure what to think. He had never heard of a condition called that, and he didn't quite know what to make of it. He looked at Blart, who was gnawing on a bone again. *Huh? Where did the cookies go? How did he get a bone again?*

That term Zombifinitis took time to sink in, but all of a sudden it hit him. *The scars, the odd color, the gnawing habit, accident-prone...* "You're a zombie!" he exclaimed, like one of those contestants on a big game show who guessed the correct answer. The mood around the table sank. It was not the big celebration he expected like at the end of the game shows. That's when what he said really sank in. He looked at Ally, then Sarah, and finally Blart. Quietly, almost to himself, as he met Blart's gaze he asked, "Wow, are you a zombie?"

Chapter 10

"First thing you need to know, Teddy, is that Blart's condition is not, I repeat, **not** contagious. Now second, Blart's condition gives him different characteristics, but Bartholomew is like any other child. He loves to do the same things any nine-year-old would love to do. His condition is extremely rare, and very little has been studied about it until recently."

Teddy was still confused and in a little awe of the whole situation. His mind was racing... *a zombie, my new friend is a zombie*, he thought. Teddy looked across the table at Blart, but this time it was different, as it all started to click into place in his mind. He had overlooked the odd color, thinking it might be a reaction to some medicine. It wasn't. The clumsiness, he thought, could have been from the height. A lot of tall people were slightly clumsy, which he concluded could lead to the exorbitant amount of scars. He had rationalized everything down to make sense, even the... "Hey! That's why you have a biting problem!" he blurted without thinking. "Well, just so you know, we're friends and I'm not lunch. You don't have to bite me."

"Teddy! It's not quite like that," Ally said, shaking her head. She thought about the few times when Blart was young that he had bitten Patches. They could never really tell if Blart bit Patches because of his condition or not. Lots of children bite until they learn it's wrong, and since then, Blart has never had another issue. "Well, not entirely like that, anyway. He does like to chew on things a lot. The doctors believe it is attributed to a nervous condition as a result of the Zombifinitis."

Teddy looked across the table at the bone hanging out of Blart's mouth. Biting people or not, Blart still had a problem. It was obvious. Teddy was also 98% sure bones to gnaw on in class were not allowed in the fourth grade. In Teddy's mind, his mission was still a necessity. *The mission... to help my new zombie friend Blart get over his biting problem.* Only one thing changed in his mind. He was now armed with the knowledge of why his new friend had a biting problem in the first place. Zombifinitis. He really wasn't sure how knowing about the condition could help. It might have just been hopefulness; but somehow, he felt like it was a big piece to the puzzle.

"There are some things you might need to know, Teddy. Some things are mild, but others can be a little extreme and might shock you." Ally managed to bring him out of his thoughts.

"Shock me?" Teddy asked.

"About the side effects of the Zombifinitis and how it has changed Blart," Ally continued. "I'll explain a little so you can understand. The mild ones are things like how Blart got his name. Shortly after we got him out of the hospital, he had to relearn a few things. Speech was less of a challenge than motor skills, but it still came with obstacles. The first few years, Blart had trouble pronouncing a lot of things, but as he seemed to master his speech, he still had problems saying his name, Bartholomew. It's not an easy name for most kids to say in the first place. He still stumbles on the first part, so most people just shorten it to Blart. We tried to correct everyone at first, but Bartholomew didn't mind. It just became easier to accept it and call him Blart. Everyone knew him as Blart anyway, so the family adopted it as his nickname. Except Sarah." She looked in her direction. "She still calls him Bart."

"It's his name, isn't it?" Sarah responded, with an edge of attitude. Teddy realized this was what Ally meant earlier when she said his name depended on whom you met first.

"Now, the extreme ones can be a little shocking, and you need to be prepared. Unlike speech, his motor skills come with a lot of challenges. He has problems with balance at times, which can lead to a lot of injuries."

Teddy focused on Blart's scars. "Yeah, he said he was accident-prone."

"Well, he has definitely had some big accidents trying to keep up with the other boys." Ally smiled with a slight chuckle. This got Blart laughing, and even Sarah joined in too.

"Remember that time you decided it was a good idea to go sledding when you didn't even know how to steer?" Sarah interjected, laughing hard. "All the kids ran home in panic when you hit the tree. Good thing too, or they would have seen you running around looking for your arm. If it hadn't crawled back, you would have had a lot more explaining to do." Sarah was laughing so hard she almost fell out of her seat, and Blart smiled so big the bone fell out of his mouth.

"Huh...**What**?" Teddy exclaimed, barely catching what she had said through the laughter. "His arm crawled back?"

Ally managed to get a hold of her laughter a little. "Extreme side effect," she said. "Nothing that couldn't be fixed with a little liquid bandage and fishing line though. It took a few trips to the store for supplies to get it on correctly, but I think he learned his lesson and slowed down a little after that. He's been a little more cautious since. Patches has the same problem. Good thing too, or we would have lost his tail and at least one ear a long time ago."

If Teddy was showing confusion before, it was minuscule to what he must be showing now. He had just jumped into full-blown insanity mode. Arms, tails, and ears crawling back? He could accept the rest but had never heard such crazy stories. Teddy started to wonder if it was all a joke. *That's got to be it. The family must be trying to pull my leg... hopefully not off, either.* "You're joking, right?" he asked. "I mean, the part about pieces crawling back."

Ally looked at Teddy. "I want you to know something, Theodore. Teddy is short for Theodore, isn't it?" He nodded in response. It was his first sign that she was completely serious. "The changes that have happened to Blart and Patches have been quite shocking to our family." She continued, "Blart is one of the most important things in our lives, and it took us a while to understand his condition. We were in as much disbelief as you, until we started noticing things. Little things at first, like his skin tone changing or always needing to chew on something, but then the odder stuff started becoming apparent. I wish I could just give you a list of side effects so you won't be shocked. The problem is, we keep finding new side effects all the time. It seems to be a big list already, and it just keeps growing. We just accept that Blart is different and we manage to do what we can when things arise."

Teddy didn't have a problem with any of it really, even strange side effects. It was just a little shocking and crazy, that's all. He had a sneaking feeling that the craziness was just beginning. Things would just get weirder, he was quite sure... a lot weirder. "Well, I don't scare easy, and I think I can handle almost anything," he commented. "If something new happens, I promise not to freak out. It's just the Zombifinitis, right?"

"Right," Ally replied.

He caught the look he got from Sarah as he said Zombifinitis. *That's right*, he thought, mouthing the words "fourth grade" to her, then "Zombifinitis". *Checkmate!*

Sarah gave him a scowl as she made another wide and obvious arc with her cookie toward the glass of milk. Dunking it extra, extra slow, she took a long bite, staring Teddy down as she finished it. When she was done, she jumped up from the table and looked directly at him with a big smile. Sarah silently mouthed the words, "overgrown toddler," then stuck out her tongue before she ran out of the dining room. Keeping score in is head, Teddy thought, *Arrgh, stalemate, not checkmate!*

Ally frowned at the exchange from Sarah. "I bet Blart would like to get to know the area a little, and besides, the unpacking isn't going anywhere. It'll still be here when Blart gets back."

Teddy looked at Blart and noticed an excitement behind his eyes. "OK, that sounds great. There's a lot to do around here. I'll show you all the best spots." Blart and Teddy got up from the table and headed out of the dining room. "First, I have to grab my backpack from your room. Maybe we can get you over that biting problem while we're at it. I brought a few things we can try."

"Soundsss gooood," Blart said with a smile. Then out of habit or nervousness, Teddy wasn't sure which, Blart put another bone in his mouth.

Chapter 11

Teddy sat down on the edge of the bed and unzipped the backpack. "I think we should start basic and see where we get." The bone was still hanging out of Blart's mouth. "First, you have to get rid of that bone. Don't worry, though. We can put it in the backpack and keep it around just in case. Remember, we are going to be fourth-graders. You can't go around chewing on a bone in the fourth grade. No one was chewing on bones in fourth grade last year, or I would have heard about that. There was a kid in second grade that ate his boogers, and I heard about that, so I would know if there was anyone chewing on bones."

Blart reluctantly took the bone from his mouth and dropped it into the backpack. "It's OK," Teddy said looking at his new friend. "We're going to figure this out together." Teddy zipped the backpack shut and stood up, slinging it over his shoulder. "Let's go outside to do this. Your mom wants me to show you around, and we need to be able to interact with others while we test our methods, or we won't know what works for biting."

Blart got up slowly and awkwardly, following Teddy to the front door. He knew he had to face fourth grade without things to bite on if bones were not allowed in class. It was strange, always wanting to bite on things. There seemed to be tension in his jaw that he just needed to get out. It built up when he got nervous. With the move yesterday and a new school year coming in just two short days, he was getting extremely nervous. His teeth started to chatter just thinking about it, causing Teddy to look back and take notice. Trying as hard as he could, Blart slowed the chattering.

Going outside, Teddy removed the first item from his pack. "Here. Put this on." Teddy handed Blart a hockey mask. "If you can't reach your mouth, you can't bite anyone. That makes sense, right?"

Blart took the mask and slowly put it on. He really didn't feel any better, but he tried it anyway.

"That's it. Now let's go to the park. It's real close, so my mom lets me go there to play."

Heading down the street, Teddy had a good feeling about their first test. Blart felt very different, though. He couldn't see very well in the mask, was moving slowly, and stepping carefully with his arms stretched out.

"It's just around the corner," Teddy said as they rounded the bend.

Blart could see slivers of metal and wood through the slits in the hockey mask, but little of anything else. There were kids playing, he could tell, because he could hear them. All of a sudden, his ears were filled with a deafening scream.

"**Monster**!!!"

It was a girl, Blart could tell from her tone, but he couldn't tell where it came from. Teddy could though, because he could see her. The girl was pointing straight at them while she was screaming.

"What? No," Teddy said, but it was too late. Other kids looked where she pointed and started screaming too. Before Teddy could say anything else, everyone started running away. "Well, that was strange." They approached the park, confused about what had just happened. Teddy looked back at Blart to

see if he needed any help. "Oh," Teddy exclaimed, then started laughing.

"Whatt isss ittt?" asked Blart, holding his arms out before him to help him balance. He could hardly see anything through the small slits of the hockey mask.

Teddy started laughing harder. He couldn't help it. In fact, Teddy laughed so hard, it took him a minute or two to catch his breath. Blart looked like someone straight out of the haunted houses during Halloween. He even resembled the crazy man on the posters advertised all over town. They were for a new scary movie at the cinema, and they looked really creepy. Unfortunately for Blart, he did too. When he finally calmed down enough, Teddy turned toward Blart. "Well, we can't have you walking around looking like that. We need to put more thought into this."

"I cannn't seee innn thisss thinnng."

Looking at Blart, Teddy suddenly got an idea. "I think maybe we should change the mask a little. It only makes sense. You can't go around looking like that guy in the movies, and besides, you can't see anyway. Here, let me see the mask." Teddy headed to a bench across the park, sat down, and reached into his bag. Pulling out some scissors, he looked at Blart. "This might take a little time, but I think it'll be better when I'm done."

It took more time than he thought. Blart managed to stumble and fall all over the park as he waited. When Teddy was finished, he had cut the top of the mask off. It looked a little better.

"Here you go. Try it now." Teddy handed back what was left of the mask.

Blart put it back on, only this time, he could see extremely well. Just the bottom half of the mask covered his face. "Thatt seeems betterrr."

"Good," Teddy responded. He had been looking around the park as Blart tried on the new mask. It was still empty. "Well, I guess we need to go somewhere else to test it." He looked over at Blart. *Oh-no, not good!* Now, Blart looked like the other poster at the cinema, the even scarier movie. "Awww, it's never going to work. It seems people are scared of hockey masks no matter how you try and cut them," Teddy said. "Maybe we should just move on and try something else."

They put the mask away, and Teddy stood up. Putting on his backpack and looking at Blart, Teddy struggled to think of what might be allowed in school for biting purposes. "I got it!" Teddy exclaimed.

"Gott whhhat?" Blart asked.

"Come on. We need to find some people to test my theory around, or we won't know if it'll help. There is a strip mall right up the road. Let's go."

Blart got to his feet and was generally excited about their tests. He never really had a friend before, not one that lasted anyway; and Teddy seemed to want to help him with his problem. Not that he felt he had a problem. *Isn't that what friends do, help one another?* Smiling big at Teddy, Blart couldn't help but get the feeling they would be close friends for a long time. "OK, I'mmmmm readddyy."

Heading down the street toward the strip mall, Blart and Teddy looked like old friends. Though they were only nine and had just met, there was a connection that just couldn't be explained. *We're like two peas in a pod... or maybe a peanut. Peanuts often have one side that grows twice the size of the other. Yeah, we're probably more like a peanut.* Teddy laughed at the thought of it. He had never thought he would meet someone he had so much in common with after Charlie moved away... *Sorry, Charlie*, Teddy thought, and that made him laugh harder. Blart looked at Teddy and raised an eyebrow. "Just a funny thought, that's all. I'll tell you about it sometime," Teddy said as they reached the shopping center.

Chapter 12

"OK, I was thinking that you could try to bite something almost everyone bites. It has to work, because they can't take them away from you at school... fingernails!" Teddy said with enthusiasm. Blart looked at Teddy with recognition behind his eyes. "I know! It's obvious." Teddy commented.

"Nottt thatt obbviousss. I neverrr thougghht of thatttt."

"Well it took me a while too," Teddy admitted, "but I know the school can't remove your fingernails, so it makes sense. There is an arcade around the corner we can start with and a bookstore we can go to as well. My mom says the arcade will rot your brain and the bookstore will build it up, but I think she's out of touch with reality. The games at the arcade are hard, and reading books is easy."

Blart laughed, "Ourrr momsss musst havve a lottt in commmmon."

"Probably more so than we think," Teddy commented. "Ok, so the way I see it is, we go in, get in the mix, and you try your best to ignore the nervousness. When you can't take it any longer, start biting on a fingernail."

"OK," Blart said.

Opening the door to the arcade, the noise hit you first. Loud beeps and sirens were going off continuously, and being the last weekend before school, it seemed like everyone was out having their last shebang of the summer. As the noise reached Teddy's ears, another noise entered the mix, the sound of chattering teeth. "It's going to be all right. Just remember, fingernails."

"Fingerrrnailssss," repeated Blart, looking at his hands. Teddy was smart to think of it. He had to be right. *They couldn't take your fingernails, could they?* With a deep breath he continued forward, making a conscious effort to stop the clacking of his teeth. Once inside, the lights and noise were overwhelming. It took a lot of self-control from him not to let his teeth smack together again.

"It's OK." Teddy was aware of his friend's struggle. "You get used to the noise pretty quick. Come on, let's watch some people play and see what happens."

Blart nodded slowly, trying to ignore the build-up of pressure in his jaw. The lights and sounds were getting to him pretty quickly. Looking at his hands, he made a conscious decision to put them in his pockets. He needed to go as long as he could without biting anything. Blart knew if he gave in too quickly, he wouldn't have any nails when he really needed them. Teddy was pretty adamant about no bones at school, so there really wasn't much of an option. It was a good suggestion, that's true. He hoped it worked, so he could at least look normal... somewhat, anyway.

Blart and Teddy moved through the arcade, looking at the games. Every one was blasting a different theme, interrupted with occasional clicks, whistles, sirens, and bleeps. Blart wondered how anyone could take the noise for long. Time seemed to lengthen, and the sounds seemed to grow louder. After a few minutes, the tension started getting extreme.

Teddy noticed the anguish in his friend's face and moved in close to whisper, "Remember, fingernails. You don't have to try and push it. Just relax and take a nibble if you need to."

Blart pulled his hands out of his pockets and looked at his nails. They were longer than most people's. It was another side effect from the Zombifinitis. They grew faster than normal, which might be good if this worked. At least his nails were always growing. Once you gnawed through a bone and it was gone, you had to get another one. This seemed like a great solution to his problem, and cheap too.

Another siren went off, making Blart jump. He got so scared his teeth started chattering instantly. Without thinking, he put his hand to his mouth, and bit down. "**Uh-Oh!**"

The sound before the "Uh-Oh" wasn't good. There was a slight snapping that didn't belong with the sounds of nail biting. Teddy looked over just in time to see Blart remove a finger from his mouth. It was wiggling in his hand back and forth, like an odd caterpillar. Teddy was mortified. He had suggested fingernails as a solution; not realizing it would become a bigger problem.

"Are you OK?" Teddy asked in total amazement. Ally had mentioned this earlier, so he wouldn't be shocked, but really? How are you not going to be shocked when unattached parts stay animated? Blart just looked at Teddy as if this was normal. In Teddy's world, this was **not** normal. Blart didn't even look like he was hurt. No expression of pain or injury, just a kid holding his wiggling finger and blinking his eyes. *How could this be normal*, he thought.

"I hope no one saw that!" Teddy exclaimed, a little shocked. He grabbed the finger as quickly as he could and stashed it in the backpack. "We had better get out of here and fix that finger of yours. I don't want your parents thinking I'm a bad influence on you, and they might, if you go home fingerless. Let's go to the convenience store. I bet they have some liquid bandage."

Blart knew his parents were very understanding about his accidents. It was always something like this that made it hard for Blart to keep any friends, though. He really hoped Teddy wouldn't get all "weird" about this. After all, he had been through much worse. Quickly hiding his four-fingered hand in his pocket, he started making his way toward the exit.

When Teddy got outside, he started laughing. Just a little at first, but after a few seconds, he was hysterical. Trying as hard as he could to speak between breaths, he managed, "Did you... I mean... did you really... I mean... did you really, really just... **bite your finger off?**"

Blart flashed his famous wonky grin and said, "Yeahhh, I diddd! Oopsss!" Teddy fell down and laughed even harder. He almost peed his pants, laughing so hard. It took quite some time for him to finally calm down.

"I'm sorry. I know it's not funny. It's just..." Teddy started laughing again.

"It'sss kinnnd of funnnyy." Blart gazed at his hand in disbelief. It was even funny to him, trying to bite a nail and missing by a mile. He inspected it for a moment, and looked back at Teddy. "Wherre doo wee gett liquid bandage?" Teddy got to his feet and pointed toward the corner. Blart looked in the direction Teddy indicated and they headed toward the store.

Teddy was smart when packing and brought money with them. He went inside the store and returned with the liquid bandage. Blart needed help setting the finger, since he really couldn't do it himself. Teddy found it a little funny that he was attaching a finger and wondered if this counted as surgery somehow. *A nine-year-old performing reattachment surgery, who would've thought it?* He understood what Ally

meant when she said a "few extra trips" to the store though, because it took a while to get it set right. This was minor compared to an arm, and it still took them 15 minutes and 3/4 of a bottle of liquid bandage to get it on correctly.

"Well, this has truly been an adventure," Teddy said. "We should probably head home before something else happens; plus, I need to brainstorm on some more ideas to help you. What do you think?"

Blart looked at his hand, stretching his reattached finger by opening and closing a fist. Teddy couldn't believe it! It was just fine and working well. Blart looked at Teddy and nodded, "Let'sss goooo."

Chapter 13

On the way home, the pair talked about fixing the telephone line. Blart had never had one, so Teddy explained how it worked. They were both sure if Blart needed any help, his dad would know exactly what to do. As for Teddy, he was an old pro. The line was originally his, and it took quite a few tries to get it right.

Teddy was determined to get it working. Since he wasn't allowed to have a cell phone, this was his way of bypassing the parents. He figured they'd be mad about it, but they weren't. Instead, everybody kept commenting about "taking them back" and "nostalgia," whatever that means. By the end of that day though, Teddy could tell you the true in and out workings of cup and string telephone systems, how to install one, and the best supplies for the job. The coolest part of the system was a separate bell they could ring in each other's rooms by shaking a second line. The sound let them know when the other was calling. Teddy explained to Blart how to install this as well.

By the time the two got back, it was close to dinner. Teddy said goodbye and reminded Blart once more about the bell system. "Be sure and listen for it. I'll call you later, and we can plan our day tomorrow."

Blart started up the drive, while Teddy made his way toward his own house. Reaching for the door, he turned back and waved to Blart. *What a crazy experience*, he thought to himself as he stepped inside. *I guess I had better prepare myself for more of the unexpected.* It was strange that what happened today didn't bother Teddy. Maybe the things Ally told him had prepared him, so he didn't react like everyone else had reacted before. That was probably it. Teddy figured if he were open to the unexpected, he wouldn't be surprised by the odd side effects. One thing he was sure of, though, was he had a great time with Blart today. They seemed to complement each other well, like best friends often do. "So what if he's a zombie. He's still cool to me," he said quietly to himself as he shut the door.

"Did you say something, Teddy?" his mom asked from the living room.

He turned around and spotted his mom sitting on the sofa with a cookbook in her hands. *Oh no, how much did she hear?* He shouldn't have said anything. "Nothing Mom, just commenting on how cool it was to meet Blart, that's all." He held his breath, wondering if she heard anything about zombies or not.

"What kinda name is Blart? I thought it was Bartholomew."

Teddy didn't respond. He really didn't know how to explain the story without telling her about the Zombifinitis. Instead, he started to sidestep toward the hall. There was a slight chance he could escape, maybe quickly slip away before she asked again.

"Oh well, it's probably just a quirky family nickname or something," she rationalized. "Are you sure it's Blart? I don't want to call him the wrong name, you know."

A nickname! It was an easy response. In fact, that's exactly what Ally said happened. He was so thrown off thinking his mom heard the comment about Blart being a zombie that he totally locked up. He couldn't think of any way to explain it. All he could think of was Zombifinitis. It was simple, really. She just needed to know it was a nickname, not the backstory on how he got it. "Yeah, it's his nickname. Everyone calls him Blart," Teddy responded. He kept inching toward the hall, ready to make a break for his room. He was so flustered he couldn't think straight.

"Well, I'm glad you two had a good time. I can't wait to meet him," his mom commented. "Maybe we can invite him over tomorrow, so your father and I will have a chance to get to know him a little."

Teddy stopped dead in his tracks. It was the obvious next step of friendship between kids. How could he not have anticipated this? He knew most parents, and especially his, would want to know who their child is friends with. His mom had already met Ally and Tom. That was good. She had never met Blart though. That could be another thing. Not that Teddy's mom was judgmental. In fact, he found her accepting of a lot of things. Zombies might not be one of them though. Teddy wasn't sure. It wasn't something she'd randomly broadcast. Plus, Teddy said he could keep a secret and planned to.

Thing was, his mom had a way of looking into him and seeing what he was hiding. Secrets were almost impossible to keep from her. She must have had some kind of "deep-secret scanner" installed in her brain; at least that's what Teddy thought. He cracked under her scrutiny on many occasions.

Not this time. Stay strong and hit her with a distraction. "Wow, it smells great in here Mom. What's for dinner? Blart and I played hard, and I'm starving." He figured if he just ignored her remark, she might not come back to it.

"Well, good. I made a lot of stuff tonight. Your dad wanted something different from me, and I know you don't want what either of us are having, so I made you something special. Why, I must have used every dish in the kitchen for tonight's dinner. I hope you like it."

Teddy was suspicious because of the overly sweet tone in her voice. "That was nice of you Mom, you really shouldn't have." The suspicion was gnawing at him deeply. He could feel something wasn't right. "It sounds like an awful lot of trouble to cook three separate dinners," he quickly added.

"No problem at all, really. I know it's the last weekend before school, and I want everyone to have a special meal." She smiled mischievously. "By the way, do you remember that little incident with your ball this morning?" The pitch she hit was indescribable. The feeling Teddy got from the tone of her voice must have been what she was after, because she smiled even bigger at his reaction. He couldn't believe it was possible to smile any bigger, but somehow, she managed it. His mom knew she hit home when his shoulders sank.

"I guess that means I have dishes to do tonight, huh?" he asked.

"That's why I didn't mind, sweetheart!" She got up from the couch and headed toward the kitchen. "It's been hard timing everything to come out together, but if all goes well, it should be ready in thirty minutes. Why don't you get cleaned up, and I will call you when it's ready."

Teddy started off toward his room thinking about his upcoming "dishcapade." Over his shoulder he heard his mom's voice one last time. "Your dad and I want to hear all about your day with the neighbors. Just call us curious, and I'm not looking for gossip either, if that's what you think."

He knew she was, or she wouldn't have added the last

part. His mom wasn't typically a gossiper, but it is a smaller town than most, and not every day do you get a new neighbor. He understood. She mostly just wanted to know what they were like. If you could carry on a conversation about what everyone in town wanted to know, you were suddenly the queen bee. In a town like this, everyone wanted to know about the new residents. Funny, it seemed he sometimes had a scanner of his own, not that a "gossiping-geese scanner" is good for anything. Shaking his head, he entered his room.

Teddy was supposed to get cleaned up for dinner, but the telephone system came first in his world. With as many dishes as his mom used, he might be tied up for most of the night. He really didn't know when it might be too late to call Blart. There was a ton of planning to do to get ready for tomorrow. He finished as fast as he could while deep in thought.

He was aware the methods they tried today didn't start out well, and ended worse. After the finger incident, Teddy decided to scrap the other options he'd planned. All he could do was get back to the drawing board. *Maybe my mom was joking about using all the dishes. Not a snow cone's chance on a schoolyard blacktop in July.* He knew he was wrong this morning, and she would be sure to make it a point.

Teddy sat down and opened his computer. *Mom said thirty minutes. That's fifteen to set up a phone, ten to research, and five to clean up. I got this!* The call for dinner came too sudden, and Teddy realized thirty minutes was more like twenty. "Be there in a sec!" he hollered as he ran to clean up.

Chapter 14

When Teddy sat down at the table, he knew immediately his mom was not exaggerating. "Did you miss anything, Mom?" Teddy asked, not trying to hide the sarcasm in his voice. It was really not a question so much as a statement.

"You do the crime, you serve the time, even if it is a delayed sentence," she responded.

Teddy slouched in his chair. Normally, he was a pretty good kid, and this was why. His mom was notorious for disciplining through chores. You can't call the authorities for chores or they'll laugh at you. He knew this, because they laughed when he called before. The fact that his dad had dialed the number should have told him something wasn't right. Things like that aren't very obvious to a five-year-old, least of all a five-year-old Teddy. Looking like he was in for a long night, all he could do was sigh.

"Did you have a good time meeting the neighbors today?" his father asked. "Because if you didn't, I have a list of things I could've used some help with." He finished the statement looking at Teddy's mother rather than Teddy. She must have shackled him with a few things while Teddy was next door. *Poor Dad, always getting cornered on his days off.* Teddy felt a little guilty for his "long weekend of watching sports" comment to his mom earlier.

"I'm sure he had a great time," his mom commented.

"In fact, I was hoping to invite the new neighbors over tomorrow, so we'd have a chance to meet everyone. What do you think, Theo?" That's what Teddy's mom called his dad. It would've been confusing if she called them the same thing. After all, the names are the same name until you reach the end. His dad was Jr. and Teddy was the III.

"Isn't that why I spent my day cleaning that old grill in the backyard?" his dad asked. "Anyway, I think it might be a good idea," he continued, not waiting for an answer. "It's hard to move to a new area surrounded by people you don't know. We should make them feel welcome and get to know them a little, especially if Teddy's going to be running around with their son." Teddy knew his dad didn't typically care about things like meeting the neighbors. He was always cordial of course, but Teddy also knew his dad would rather spend his day focusing on twenty obscure sports channels. Not that his dad wasn't social. In fact, he could be the life of the party. He just didn't fill up his time with social activities as much as his mom did.

"I don't know, Mom. They just moved in, and it's one day before school starts. They probably have a lot to do." Teddy knew his mom wanted to meet the new family, but how would they react to Blart? He really liked hanging out with Blart, and if his parents knew he had Zombifinitis, they might not let him. Obviously, Blart's condition made him different, and that could raise a lot of questions depending on what someone sees. If his parents had witnessed the finger incident earlier, Teddy would never have been able to explain it. That would've led to a whole slew of other problems.

Teddy didn't know what to do, but it wasn't his place to really do or say anything. He made a promise to keep a secret, and he planned to do it. If his parents plan a get-together with the neighbors tomorrow, he'll just deal with things as they arise. Teddy's attitude suddenly changed. This might be what he needed before school, a practice run. If they could keep a secret tomorrow, he would definitely be able to keep it in a school environment.

"Who knows? They might like to come-over," he quickly added.

"I certainly hope so. All we can do is ask," his mom commented. "I'll go over and invite them after dinner. Is it just the three of them?"

"No, they have a daughter named Sarah too. She's kind of a handful," Teddy admitted. This got a laugh out of his father. "She kept calling me an oversized toddler. I don't know how Blart handles it. A sister would drive me crazy."

His dad smiled. "Well, now seems like a perfect time as any to break the news. What do you think, Joyce?"

Teddy got a look of sheer horror on his face. *What!!! Was he about to be a brother? Noooooo!!!*

"Theo! Quit teasing your son!" his mom scolded, chuckling a little. Teddy relaxed but still seemed a little suspicious.

"Sorry, but did you see the look in his eyes? Priceless!" his Dad hooted. "What kinda name is Blart anyway? Joyce, I thought you said it was Bartholomew."

Teddy always had a hard time telling when his dad was kidding. His timing was too impeccable, and Teddy was extremely gullible according to his dad. He realized he'd have to start making a conscious effort to work on that.

"When are you planning to have them over? Blart and I have big plans tomorrow," Teddy asked, ignoring his dad's remarks.

"Really, what plans?" his mom asked.

Uh-oh, he couldn't let them know the specifics. He thought about it quickly. "Just getting a few things ready for Blart, so he'll be prepared for school, that's all." *Whew, close one.* Teddy figured if he stayed with generalities, he wouldn't have to explain the whole situation.

"Preparation is important," his dad managed between mouthfuls, not bothering to look up. He shoved in a few more bites then managed to raise his head toward Teddy. "So I hear you two are going to be in class together. Should be good for him to already know somebody, so he doesn't have to feel alone in a big new school. I hope he's 'on the up and up' though. You and Charlie used to get a little too curious, if you know what I mean," he said with a raised eyebrow. Mom raising an eyebrow meant suspicion. Dad raising an eyebrow meant, "Do you get it?" Teddy thought how strange it was that the same facial expression, from two different people, would often mean two completely different things.

It was true that Charlie and Teddy spent a ton of time in trouble from their curiosities, but that was mostly when they were five. They really shaped up over the last couple of years, although they still had a few missteps, so to speak. "I know, but Blart is different than Charlie." Teddy thought back to the sled story and the finger incident. "Blart seems a little... well... I can't say for sure, but I think he's a little less *curious,*" he added.

"All boys are curious," his mom cut in. "Curiosity kills the cat, and little boys' social lives too. It was curiosity that made you climb that fence earlier, young man." Teddy knew it wasn't a stab at him so much as a point. He had spent numerous hours grounded due to his own curiosity. She was right, and because of it, he was on dish duty tonight.

"What are the neighbors like?" his father changed the

subject.

Teddy actually started to get excited. "Well, I never got to meet his dad, Tom, but Ally was extremely nice. I think you'll both like her. Sarah, like I explained before, is a typical pain and a half. If you don't want to invite her, I would totally understand..."

"Theodore!" his mom's voice cut in.

"Sorry. Blart is into the same stuff I am. We both have a lot of things in common." Teddy continued to tell his parents as much as he could about his day with the neighbors and what they were like. He tried his best not to keep saying bad things about Sarah, though he did get a couple more "Theodore!" interruptions from his mom.

While they were clearing the table for Teddy's dish party, his mom decided to drop by the neighbors' house. He was still washing the dishes as his mom returned with an excited tone in her voice. He couldn't quite hear what his parents were saying over the water, so he turned it off.

"Well, that'll be great," he heard his dad say from the other room.

"I just know we are going to have a great time. I really miss the weekends we used to have with Susan, Dean, and Charlie."

"I know, Joyce. I bet if Blart really is anything like Teddy, chances are his parents are probably a lot like us."

"Oh, I hope you're right, Theo. It's hard to say, talking to them so briefly, but I get a good feeling from Ally, and I think you might really like Tom." His mom's voice was getting louder. "What do you think we should make?"

Teddy turned the water back on as she entered the kitchen with his dad in tow.

"I really don't know. I thought I could swing by the

grocery store in the morning and pick something up. Should we stick with burgers and hot dogs, or go with something else like barbecue chicken?"

Teddy kept washing while he listened to his parents discuss what should be on the menu. Something kept nagging at the back of his mind as he listened to them discuss the best things to serve tomorrow. An image of Blart flashed through his head, so Teddy looked back at his parents. He had the perfect suggestion. "How about ribs?"

Chapter 15

Next door, Blart and his dad were in the process of finishing the telephone line. Tom had managed to find an old coffee can and promised it was the best thing to use for proper reception. It was funny to Blart, that he could use an old coffee can as a telephone. He really didn't understand the principle behind it yet, but his dad said it was quite simple. The string had to be tight for it to work, then sound could travel through the string and echo in the coffee can. Blart was a little skeptical but was excited to give it a try.

The move had been pretty fortunate for him so far. It was cool to have a kid next door his own age, but to Blart, the fact that Teddy seemed to look past his Zombifinitis meant so much more. He was close to two years old when he contracted it, so memories before that were very foggy. He did however remember the several months he spent in the hospital afterward.

Things really started to change when he got out. He never really felt different, since being like this was all he could really remember anyway. The changes seemed to come from others. Whenever something outside the "norm" happened, and *outside the "norm"* being someone else's *"norm,"* people stopped coming around. They would make excuses as to why their kids couldn't come over and play, the most outrageous excuses sometimes. Blart was always aware of why though. It was funny how people thought he was slow because of his

clumsiness and the way he talked, but he was quite smart. Probably due to the amount of time he spent alone. He liked to read a lot. It was something he could do by himself.

Changes in people and their reaction to Blart started becoming extremely apparent after he went through a stint of trying to impress the neighborhood kids. Instead of impressing them, he ended up scaring most of them half to death. He couldn't get anyone to come by after that. The parents' reaction to him was even more brutal. They would hug their kids extra close as he'd pass by, as if he couldn't see the subtleties of the situation. Like he didn't have eyes or feelings. That's the problem with most parents, they view kids as... well, kids. They believe kids can't comprehend most situations. This time might be a little different. Teddy didn't seem to shock too easily. He had already reattached a finger, and instead of running away horrified, he just laughed. It was one of the more shocking aspects of his condition, and Teddy took it like it was a normal situation. There was a comforting feeling in that.

"Isss ittt readyyy?" Blart's excitement was obvious.

"Just finishing the inside knot."

"Thanksss, Daaad."

"I just think it's neat that this string system is even here. It's like a dinosaur in today's technology. I would've never suspected it was a telephone line, even though I had one when I was a kid. You're going to be amazed at how well it works. I can't believe it, they even installed a bell so you know when a call is coming. Teddy did this?"

"Yeahhh, hee cann't gett a phonne unntill hee reeachesss doubbllle digitsss. Hee innstallled thiss innsteaad, Prettyyy cooool, huhh."

"Pretty cool," his dad repeated, looking at Blart's smile.

It made him happy to see Blart with so much excitement. He was a little worried Teddy and his family might not be able to understand Blart's full condition though. Tom didn't know about Ally's talk over milk and cookies earlier, or even the finger incident. He just didn't want to see Blart hurt again when things got a little strange, as they often did.

"The neighbors invited us over tomorrow for an afternoon cookout, kind of a last day of summer get together. Should be fun. What do you think?"

Blart was excited but a little horrified at the same time. He knew he would have to meet Teddy's parents. That's how things worked. That was also how things outside *the* "norm" happened. Blart's jaw started chattering. He couldn't help it, even if he wanted to. Some people sweat when they're nervous, but for him, his teeth chattered.

"Look, we don't have to go if you don't want to, but I think it might be a good idea. We already accepted the invite, but we could cancel."

"Nooo, it'sss OK," Blart said through chattering teeth as he picked up a new bone. Blart knew Teddy wasn't going to be a problem, he could tell. He'd just have to make a conscious effort to impress the parents, that's all, or at the least not scare them to death.

The bell started chiming. "Looks like you have a call. Remember to hold it with the string tight or you won't be able to hear. I'll leave you to it." His dad headed out of the room.

Blart picked up the can and pulled it tight with a little doubt about the whole setup. He figured he'd try it anyway. After all, it worked for Teddy and that kid Charlie. "Hellooo," he said into the can.

"Looks like we are having a barbecue tomorrow," Teddy's voice came through, almost startling Blart. He wasn't expecting it to sound so clear. It had a little hollowness and echo to it, but it was clear.

"Yeahhh. I'mmm Nervousss." Blart hoped Teddy could hear his response. Being a novice to the string telephone system, Blart wasn't sure if he was using it right. Teddy's voice echoed through the can again setting Blart at ease. His dad was right. He was amazed that it worked.

"I just think of it as practice before school. If we can maintain tomorrow, school will be a breeze. You don't have to worry about my parents either; just be yourself. They love me, and you and I are a lot alike. They've got to like you, you'll see."

"I hhope sooo," Blart responded as he reached over and opened up his computer. His dad had helped him move his desk when he showed him the phone line. "You've got to put your phone on your desk," he told him. "That's how the professionals do it." Blart spoke through the phone again as the computer started booting, "Doo you waant tooo playyy a gaame?"

"I hoped you'd ask. I already have my computer on."

"Howww aabout Spacccce Fighterrr Threeee," Blart suggested.

"Logging in now," came the response.

Blart smiled again, and with the game, his nerves started melting away. Teddy was quite good, and they made it through eight levels before they had to save their mission. "Gooood Niiight, Teddddyy," Blart said through the phone as he shut off the computer.

"Good night, Blart. I'll see you tomorrow."

With that, Blart set down the phone and reflected on his day. He managed to make a friend, bite off a finger, scare a park full of kids, gnaw through a bone, and all the while,

Teddy stayed and helped. His day was awesome and the most fun he had had in a long time. Blart drifted off to sleep thinking about his newest friend, a little less worried about the next day.

Chapter 16

The morning time at Teddy's house was frantic. His dad had already been to the store twice. Teddy thought he must have avoided his own advice about planning, or he would've never had to go the second time. It might have been different if Teddy had been allowed to go with him but his mom needed help with the house. Between the cleaning and the setup for the barbecue, Teddy lost track of time. It was almost two o'clock and the neighbors would arrive shortly, but Teddy wasn't any closer in his research to help Blart. His time had been planned meticulously by his mom, which left very little for his own agenda. When his mom told him to go clean up, he had no choice but to rush through his research.

After opening page after page of parenting techniques on preventing biting in children, Teddy's eyes started to cross. He moved into suggestions that applied to animals, but nothing seemed appropriate to try on Blart. There were suggestions on muzzles, confinement, and discipline.

Teddy looked at the discipline suggestions but didn't think a rolled-up newspaper was the best thing to try in this circumstance. In fact, they were mostly designed to stop biting as an attack. Hitting a nose was supposed to work for both dogs and sharks, which surprised Teddy as he read it, but the suggestion for things like whips and chairs used to train tigers really threw him for a loop. Thinking about someone in a tank trying to swat a shark nose was bad enough. Thinking about

someone with a whip and chair surrounded by lions just seemed crazy. Teddy could understand how the whip could help, but what was the chair for? It made no sense. Teddy was pretty sure a biting tiger wasn't in the mood to sit down.

Looking more into confinement, he noticed suggestions about kennels and cages. Teddy thought about Blart in class with a cage surrounding him made out of chicken wire and coat hangers. *He'd never be able to sit down. They'd have to prop him against a wall because he wouldn't fit in a desk.*

Teddy kept looking and came across the suggestions of using chains. *Blart would definitely be able to sit down with a chain*, he thought, *but what if he had to use the restroom? Wouldn't it cross a line with the protection agencies to chain a kid to his desk? Did that really solve the problem of biting or just prevent it from happening? That solution might just compound their problems.*

Teddy rubbed his temples. This was not going as smoothly as he thought it would. *Solving a biting problem could be an overwhelming challenge,* Teddy started to think to himself. He figured he wouldn't even look at the muzzle pages after their experience at the park yesterday. *If you put a person in a muzzle, you might as well give them a sign to hold that says, "Be scared of me! I'm not normal!"*

He seemed to be getting nowhere. "What else can help cure biting problems?" he mumbled to himself. Discipline and confinement were quickly getting crossed off the list of options. He had this nagging feeling there had to be something else. What was it? There was something he was missing about the situation.

He suddenly got the thought maybe it was a dental issue. Excited again, Teddy started looking at dental pages about biting problems. It seemed the "big fix" for that issue involved rectifying one's teeth. He wasn't sure how that would help. *I have someone with a biting problem,* he thought. *Oh really, maybe we should give him better teeth to bite with.* Shaking his head, Teddy decided to bypass that option too.

He started to wander across page after page with no idea what to look for anymore. He still had that nagging feeling he was looking at things all wrong. As he moved from one page to another, he could see that this was not helping. Teddy started thinking about the true issue. *It wasn't that Blart bit people.* At least, that's what Ally told him. *Blart needed to gnaw on things. That in a nutshell could get someone in trouble, especially if you chose to chew on the wrong things. Charlie had a dog they named Shredder because of his gnawing talent with the family slippers, and Shredder was always in trouble.*

The biting problem seemed to morph in Teddy's mind the more he thought about it. *There was still the potential of biting. After all, Blart was still a zombie. Now, though, the problem became biting compounded by gnawing. It was starting to look more like a chewing problem.* This was definitely getting a little confusing for Teddy and his approach to his research. The doorbell rang, bringing Teddy out of his thoughts and back to the present. "Well, I guess we'll have to play this by ear then," he mumbled. He had a few things left from his previous research, though the more he thought about them, the more he was skeptical any would work for Blart's condition. After a day with Blart, Teddy didn't feel like being bitten was much of a threat at all, but they still needed to work it out, just in case. With that thought, Teddy ran to open the door.

Chapter 17

"I'm so glad you could make it!" his mom's voice rang out over his shoulder. "Please come in."

Teddy held his breath as his mom ushered the neighbors into the living room. Teddy noticed a slight clicking sound coming from Blart as they entered. *They're just your typical family with two kids*, Teddy thought to himself, *if typical means one of your kids is a zombie. It's only a barbecue, what could go wrong?*

"Theo, the neighbors are here," his mom called toward the kitchen.

His dad entered the living room for the round of introductions. "I was just finishing up with the food. I hope you like ribs." He made his way across the room. "I'm Theo, as I'm sure you just heard. It's very nice to meet you." His dad whisked up Tom's hand and gave it a shake. He made his way toward Ally with the same gesture.

"This is Blart, and this is Sarah," Ally motioned toward the kids. Teddy could still hear the clicking sound coming from Blart. His dad never seemed to notice as he grabbed the kids' hands and gave them each a shake. He didn't even seem to notice the scars on Blart's hand. "Wow, you're only nine?" Teddy's dad was taking-in Blart's size.

"What do you think, Joyce? I bet Blart could be an underwater hockey champion, don't you?" His dad looked at him up and down, "I mean, you look like you're built for sports." Blart's teeth almost went into overdrive by the sound of it, but Theo was totally oblivious.

Teddy's mom was looking around the room with a strange expression on her face. "Do you hear that, Theo?" She kept looking around, trying to peg the sound. Teddy caught Blart's eye. He saw Blart try and clamp his jaw tighter; but each time he pressed down, it would make the sound rev up like a motorcycle. It took every bone in Teddy's body not to laugh. It was a ridiculous sight if you knew where the sound was truly coming from. His mom was wandering back and forth everywhere, trying to figure it out. She even looked outside the window a couple of times.

"Is it me? Theo? Do you hear that?"

"Huh? Hear what?"

"That noise. It's a strange tapping, clacking. I don't know. You don't hear that? It keeps getting faster and slower, like a strange motor."

His dad cocked his head and strained to listen. Tom and Ally exchanged looks and were about to say something, when his dad dismissed the sound. "It's probably something knocking around in the air conditioner, like a belt, or a loose drum. Nothing to worry about though, I can look at it later."

His mom was still looking around the room. "Are you sure, Theo? I haven't heard it before."

Teddy cut in as fast as he could. "Can I show Blart my room?" Teddy grabbed Blart by the arm and headed toward the hall, not waiting for a response. As they walked out of the room, he heard his dad, "See, Joyce? It stopped. Nothing to worry about."

"Whew, that was close," Teddy said as they headed down the hallway. Teddy was a little frazzled, and the neighbors had only just arrived. Blart's biting problem needed

to go to the back burner for now. They had bigger issues to attend to.

Teddy was pretty sure his parents might overreact to the Zombifinitis condition, if they knew the truth. He hadn't been prepared for his mom's reaction to the sound of Blart's jaw clacking together. How could he miss that? He should have known Blart would be nervous. If it hadn't been for his dad's dismissal, Teddy was confident his mom would have pegged the sound's origin. What were they going to do? It was a fine line to walk, especially with his mom. The sound of Blart's teeth beating together finally quieted down as they entered Teddy's room.

"Wowwww!"

Blart's reaction said it all. Teddy had worked extra hard on his room after he turned seven. All the toddler stuff had been removed upon his insistence. He was always getting misjudged because of his size, so there was no need to provide extra ammo. That had been his argument when he went to ask his parents; but to his surprise, his parents had loved the idea. "You shouldn't hold onto things you don't use anymore," they commented at the time. After two years of overhaul, he had perfected his surroundings.

There were posters meticulously hung upon the wall, models set upon the desk, his Action Hero bed sheets (of course), and then there was his pride and joy. Every episode of Action Hero Crime Fighters, episodes 1-135, was tucked in perfect chronological order into his bookshelf. There was a special image printed on the spine of each one, so when you had them in order, a scene appeared. Very few people had ever seen the full scene. You had to be a serious collector, like Teddy.

"That'sss coool! I've neverrr seeen thatt!" Blart

exclaimed when he spotted it.

"Well, take it in, my friend," Teddy responded, "you have just joined the ranks of the top 2% in the Action Hero Crime Club. Few have seen it in its entirety."

Blart continued to look around the room, so Teddy sat down and continued to work out the problem of how to hide Blart's condition. It was going to be difficult. That was obvious. The food would be served soon, so they didn't have much time before they'd have to face his parents again. Teddy started laughing.

"What'sss sooo funnyyy?" Blart asked.

Teddy looked up. "Trying to hide a zombie from your own parents... who does that?"

"You'rre nott realyyy hidinnng a zombieee, jusst my connditionnn," Blart reminded him. "Myyy parentsss havvve somme experiencccce, jusst followww theirr leeead."

"You two are pathetic!" Sarah's voice cut through from the doorway. "Don't you know parents always overlook the obvious?" Sarah entered the room with a scrutiny behind her voice while shaking her head. Eyeballing Teddy, she leaned real close. "It's a lot like your room. If you get rid of the baby stuff, maybe no one will think you're a baby." *She was too much. How did Blart put up with her?* "Same thing," she continued. "just avoid the major zombie problems and your parents will overlook the rest. They can't question anything or it would be rude, so they have to accept the little odd stuff. The only thing left is rationalizing it down in their own minds, coming to some form of reason and acceptance. Gosh, you have a lot to learn. Are you positive you're not a giant four-year-old?"

Teddy just stood and blinked his eyes for a second. "All those big words, and you can't say Zombifinitis?" he smirked.

She was right. He knew it. His parents wouldn't be able to ask anything without looking rude, so the answer was obvious. Just act natural. What else could he do? He looked at Blart and Sarah, realizing he was more worried about this than they were. "OK, I get it. If you act like nothing is wrong, people are less likely to question, because they are afraid they might insult you. Sounds logical."

"It only works if you avoid the major stuff," she said again.

"What falls under major stuff?"

"With Blart? Just about anything!" She took off down the hall, laughing.

"Hey! What do you mean?" Teddy called after her, but she didn't hear him. He turned back to Blart. "You must be a saint. If you do have to bite something today, I hope it's your sister."

Blart laughed. "I thhhink sheee likess you," he said, laughing harder. "I meann shee reaaalllllyyyyy likess you."

The sound of Blart stretching out the word "really" was incredibly comical to Teddy. It was almost too long, unnaturally long. It almost sounded like... well, like Blart was a zombie. Teddy started laughing too as he heard it. They were almost in tears when they heard a voice ring through the house, "Time for lunch!"

Chapter 18

As the pair made their way down the hall, there was a certain quiet that gnawed at the back of Teddy's mind. He was having trouble placing it, when he suddenly realized what it was. "Hey," he commented, "your teeth aren't clacking." It was the lack of sound that tipped him off.

Blart smiled. "I guesss the nervves are gettting bettterr."

The truth was really quite simple. Blart was starting to realize he felt totally comfortable around Teddy. He wasn't so nervous when Teddy was around. It's true he was nervous about meeting Teddy's parents, but he figured anyone would be nervous about that. Everyone wants to give a good first impression. What calmed him down was Teddy had proved he could be a true friend, knowing that helped him relax a ton.

Teddy was accepting of Blart's condition. There was a certain liberating feeling on his nerves to feel he might not have to explain something under scrutiny. It seemed funny to Blart the more he thought about it. The nervousness he tended to feel was directly related to the thought of having to explain about his nervous condition, which made him more nervous. It was just a vicious nervous loop.

With Teddy it was different. He proved awesome in helping during a crisis, like the arcade incident. It helps to know you have someone by your side. That in a nutshell, had a certain calming effect of its own.

Teddy opened the door; outside, the smell in the air was

outrageous. Teddy's mouth started watering instantly. Ribs!

The patio was at once a scene of chaos and hysteria. Ally, Joyce and Theo were out of breath gathered around the table. Sarah was jumping up and down clapping in the middle of the yard, while Tom was by the fence with an odd look on his face.

Clack... clack. Teddy looked over his shoulder at Blart who shook his head, "Nott fromm mee." Another sound tore through the air. "Grrrarrk! Grrrarrk! Grrrarrk! GrrrGrrrGGrrGGGGrrrrarrrrk!"

Patches was on the other side of the fence going nuts. The sound was so insistent that Teddy could almost tell what Patches was trying to communicate. *Ribs! Ribs! Ribs! Can't you tell?* **I want ribs** ! It sounded funny. Teddy was suddenly hit with the realization everyone around the table was out of breath from laughing.

Clack... clack. "Here... he... goes again..." his dad said between breaths, pointing toward the fence. Teddy spun around in time to see Patches above the fence line, like he was bouncing on a trampoline. His ears were flying wildly, and he was trying to lick the air between barks.

"Grrrarrk! GrrrGrrrGGrrGGGGrrrrarrrrk!"

"I still can't figure out how he's doing that." Tom was trying his best to look through the cracks in the fence while Sarah jumped up and down, continuing to clap beside him.

"He must really like ribs," Joyce commented while trying to hold it together. "You should take him a few bones later."

Ally caught her breath. "Tom, come sit down. He seems fine. He'll probably tire himself out... eventually." She started with a new round of laughter.

"OK. It smells delicious, just ask Patches," Tom answered

while pointing over his shoulder. Patches was in the air again, twisting and licking, his tongue flying from side to side as he tried to get a taste of anything. That sent the whole table into more laughter, including Blart and Teddy.

They started into lunch, trying their best to ignore Patches. The conversation quickly changed to school between Ally and his mom, while Tom and his dad talked about work. Teddy couldn't talk. The ribs were the only thing on his mind. Picking up a rib and getting ready for his first bite, he caught a flash of motion out of the corner of his eye. A streak really, because the motion was so fast, it became a blur. A nanosecond later the real chaos exploded.

Tom's voice cut through the air. **"Patches! No!"** but it was too late. Patches was already leaping through the air by Teddy's head. Landing on the table, Patches made a skidding turn right toward the rib Blart had in his mouth.

Jumping up awkwardly from his seat, Blart clamped down tight upon the bone and braced himself. Patches had to take a leap of faith off the edge of the table to get what he was after, but as he flew through the air, he managed to twist just enough to get his jaw on his target. Swinging, growling, and hanging from the end of the bone, the scene was surreal. Teddy's mom gasped, and his dad almost choked. Blart twisted from side to side with Patches still hanging onto the bone with determination. The initial shock melted away, at least for Teddy, and he started laughing at the sight of it.

"Patches, stop that!" Ally scolded. Her voice was loud, but it was lost in the sound of chaos. "Patches!" she tried again; but still, it had no effect. Patches was attached to that bone and not letting go. Before anyone realized what was happening, Blart was already on the ground squaring off with Patches. In the next instant, the most outrageous Tug of War

game ever witnessed by Teddy began to commence.

Just act natural and they'll overlook the little stuff. The words kept ringing over and over in his head as he watched the scene unfolding before him. He couldn't help it. His laughter grew louder and louder as the phrase kept repeating and repeating. *What would ever constitute as little stuff with Blart?* Teddy wondered. *I must be going crazy.* What came next wasn't just crazy; it was an absolute shock.

"Wow! I'm telling you, Blart's a natural athlete! Look at that!" Theo said as Blart and Patches grappled over the bone, both clamped down and neither letting go.

"Huh?" Teddy was genuinely confused. Luckily, the noise of the Tug of War struggle drowned out his vocalized shock.

"It's absolutely sweet that Blart plays with Patches that way," Joyce commented to Ally.

"HUH?" The sound escaped Teddy again, only louder this time. He couldn't help it. His parents kept throwing him for loops with their responses.

"What was that, honey? Did you say something?" his mom asked, turning toward Teddy.

"Just cheering on Blart, that's all," he responded. Teddy had to stop reacting that way! Taking a deep breath, he focused himself. *Just act natural and they'll overlook the little stuff,* he thought, looking at his zombie friend on the ground, fighting over a bone with his zombie dog. *In what world would this ever constitute "little stuff?"*

"OK," she said dismissively, turning back toward Ally.

He couldn't believe it. She didn't even question him. He had actually put some thought into his statement before he answered. *Maybe that's why she let it go.* The thought was simple; *embrace the madness as if it was normal. It was amazing! The oddest of odd things going on right in front of my parents, and not a single question. Maybe Sarah was right.*

Blart finally let go, and Patches tore off at lightning speed with his prize, his tail flopping wildly back and forth as he ran. Dusting off his clothes, Blart returned to the table with a grin. The funniest part of the whole thing was that people truly saw what they wanted to see. Teddy had only been around Blart for a little more than a day. He had already seen a multitude of ungraceful accidents; yet his dad saw Blart's size and translated that into power, grace, and strength in his mind. Teddy tried his best to hide the shock in his eyes as his Dad started into it again.

"Tom, did you play any sports growing-up? I mean; he had to get those genes from somewhere, right? Don't be modest now."

"Well, I had a pretty good run at a scholarship for the backwards triathlon. I held the record in the 1000 meter crab crawl."

"I knew it! Did you hear that, Joyce? That's where Blart gets it. Now Tom, I know he is just going into the fourth grade, but it's never too young to get him involved. The schools don't start programs until seventh grade, but we have great community leagues in the area."

His mom was only halfway listening, Teddy could tell. She had that questioning look in her eye he knew all too well, like she was analyzing something in her mind that didn't quite make sense. She shook her head and returned to the conversation at hand. Something in Teddy made him question what she might be correlating. He might be dodging a lot of questions later tonight. She was just too intuitive. Teddy still couldn't help feeling the situation was a ticking time bomb. He returned half of his focus back to eating, stealing long side-glances at her when he could. The other half of his focus was still tumbling and reeling with the shock of the whole situation. He knew his parents, and things weren't quite adding up in his mind. *Dad, well... not really out of the "norm"*. Although his dad was incredibly smart, he tended to overlook a lot of things. Teddy didn't necessarily think it was because he didn't see things around him, he just thought it was because his dad tended to see things in a different light. Teddy was pretty sure no matter what happened with Blart, his dad might never see the real situation. That put him a little more at ease. He would probably only have to focus on one front, his mom.

He looked across the table at his newest friend. Blart was clumsily accident-prone, slightly green, scarred in a multitude of places, with reattached appendages and a wonky grin. Combine all that with the strange occurrences Patches adds to the mix, and he was pretty sure his mom had a laundry list of questions building inside her mind. Although she made it seem like she was overlooking everything, Teddy knew she really wasn't. Teddy took a deep breath, trying to shake the feeling he was getting.

To Teddy's surprise, the lunch seemed to go pretty smoothly after all. Patches was lying down in the grass gnawing away, quite content with the new bone he won. The pile of rib bones was stacking heavily on Blart's plate, and quickly too. That brought a few championship eating comments from Teddy's dad. Theo was pushing the idea that there was a whole league out there. You could enter any event you want, from the typical hot dog to the extreme grub-chomping challenges. He kept insisting someone like Blart could always eat free if he planned a circuit of restaurant challenges.

Teddy started relaxing a little more, and the uneasy feeling of facing his mom started to fade. She and Ally were discovering they had a lot in common, and were laughing together in their own little world. Teddy was surprised at their commonalities. Blart said it sounded like their moms were a lot alike. *Maybe the neighbors moving here would be good for the whole family. They really seemed to be getting along well, even Sarah*, Teddy thought as he looked her way.

Sarah was a mess, from head to toe. There seemed to be more barbecue sauce on her face than on the ribs. She'd even managed to get it streaked into her hair. Trying to use the back of her hand as a napkin, she wasn't succeeding in anything but smearing more sauce on her face. *That was the difference between second-graders and fourth-graders, eating experience.*

Sarah looked up and caught Teddy's eye as she pulled her hand across her mouth again. He couldn't help himself. He picked up a rib carefully with the tips of his fingers, so as not to make a mess, and took a bite. Carefully dabbing the corners of his mouth with his napkin, he tried to display some sophistication. *That's right, drink it in. Fourth-graders have sophistication, unlike messy second-graders.* The look he got back from her said it all... but it was so worth it.

Chapter 19

When lunch was finished, the cleanup started. As the leftovers were being wrapped, his dad disappeared to the garage and returned with a box. "Hey, look what I found," he declared, holding it out before him. Teddy looked up to see his dad with a box of yard games. It was the "Mongo Ultra Deluxe Outdoor Game Set" that Teddy had pointed out at the store once before. It had Lawn Darts, Horseshoes, Table Pong, Badminton, Ring Toss, Lawn Bowling, and Bolo; all in one packaged set with a carrying case so you won't lose the pieces. To top it off, the "Mongo Set" came with an extra compartment on the back that doubled as a cooler. You could fill it with sodas and snacks, and play all day with no worries.

"Whoa!" Blart exclaimed.

Teddy couldn't have said it any better. He had nagged his dad about it many times during the spring. *"Please Dad, please. Charlie and I could really use it this summer. You're the one who says we need to be more active. Please?"* Little did Teddy know that Charlie was going to move away, and it would end up a very lonely summer. He stopped asking for the game set when he found out about the move. What was he going to do with it then? Stare at it? Set up games for two or more players, then run back and forth trying to play by himself? It wouldn't make any sense to get it after Charlie moved. He had put it out of his mind, but now that Blart was next door... His dad was the best.

"I saw it at the store this morning, and it was the last one on the shelves. I just couldn't pass it up." His dad gave him a wink. "I was thinking it might be fun to set up and play a few games."

Joyce manipulated the puzzle of items in the fridge, trying to make more space for the leftovers. "Why don't you take Tom and the kids outside and get things ready while Ally and I finish in here," she said over her shoulder. Teddy was suspicious, so he moved slowly toward the door, trying to hang around.

"The boys seem to be bonding well. I have a feeling we might be in for some roller-coaster rides with those two," Joyce commented to Ally, as she forced another container into the fridge.

Ally smiled. She couldn't help but think of the roller-coaster ride she'd been on since Blart's diagnosis. What Joyce said really hit the nail on the head for her. She was about to respond as Joyce mentioned, "I'm glad you have been so accepting and nice to Teddy. After jumping the fence yesterday, it could have gone very differently for him. Another neighbor might have chased him off, like bitter old Mr. Taylor on the corner." She jerked her thumb over her shoulder, indicating the direction. "I'm sure you'll get a chance to meet," she laughed. "Just be prepared. He's a little eccentric and uptight. You know the type. He yells at you to get off the grass when you're on the sidewalk."

Ally chuckled. "Back in the city, we had this one neighbor that hung out in his pajamas on his stoop. He would yell at people randomly if they were anywhere on the street. He did it so often, I got the impression it was his hobby."

"Must have been Mr. Taylor's brother," Joyce commented.

Teddy heard their exchange as he stood in the doorway, eavesdropping on their conversation. He knew his mom. This was surface level. He was not sure what direction she would go and was worried she might try to start digging. Having everyone go outside was her way of isolating Ally for a deeper conversation, he knew. There was no way he could leave her alone, he knew that too, especially after all the craziness during lunch. What was he going to do?

His mom was so different from his dad, a little quieter, but always analyzing the world around her. She saw a lot more than surface level. It's like she had a radar that could peg you doing wrong a mile away and super-bionic ears that could hear you doing something wrong from the other room. She could wash dishes with Theo watching TV at full volume and still manage to hear the hum of a computer that shouldn't be on, because "someone" should be in bed sleeping. Teddy knew this, because it happened more than you think. Scariest of all was the sonar. She could look right through you, bounce her secret waves out her eyes, and they return with information she shouldn't have. It was unnerving. When she gave you that look, her eyes signaled you were about five seconds from having to backpedal your explanation, and about ten seconds from stammering around wanting to change the subject. Trying to avoid it never worked either. You might feel like it worked, if the timing for a deeper sonar-scan wasn't right. It was never that simple though, because she could rescan you at any time. You didn't even have to be present. Like her sonar had the ability to go into a deep time loop, focusing back to the original situation, then blindside you when you thought you got away with it. The delayed double sonar-scan. It was the ultimate in an arsenal of "super-power" mom abilities.

Teddy had a feeling he might be dealing with her sonar

later, especially if any more odd situations happened. The chances for odd situations seemed to increase in direct proportion to the time one spent with Blart. That was Teddy's "super power," knowing when he was about to have to face his mom's super powers. He'd feel it deep down, with a sense of dread, like a knot building in his gut. It was more like an early warning system than any real power, because it never really helped Teddy. In fact, he complained once to his dad about his stomach hurting while his mom scrutinized him with peering eyes. His dad laughed and told him it was his own guilty feelings gnawing away at him from the inside. It really wasn't guilty feelings; he could feel it under her scrutiny even when he had nothing to hide. It was definitively an early warning system; and with the way he was starting to feel, it was going off like an air-raid siren through his body and head. Every system he had was sounding off. A public announcement was ringing in his ears. *Alert... alert... code red, repeat, code red... we have moved to level one... imminent danger.* He didn't need to get tied up in knots now; that would almost be a dead giveaway. She had already glanced his way a few too many times, and he was quite sure she was already super-scanning him in every way.

"Did you need anything, Teddy?" she asked. "I thought you were going outside to set up the games with your Dad. Did you want to help us with the cleanup instead?" Joyce knew her question would be effective. She raised her eyebrow for a little extra push. That maneuver always worked.

Teddy saw the look. He knew it was a trap. If he stayed she would be suspicious, and he had no idea what level of suspicion she was already at. He knew any typical kid would be excited and running outside to play. That was the normal and expected thing to do. His lingering was already drawing suspicion. He had been acting like he was just moving slowly, but it wasn't fooling his mom. If he left, he would have no idea what his mom was about to dig for. Teddy knew her. She had that sly way of controlling a conversation to get info you didn't even realize you were providing. It was unnerving.

Trapped into a corner, he didn't know what to do. She was up to something, and if his mom found out about the Zombifinitis, Teddy was sure the outcome wouldn't be favorable. His mom wasn't judgmental, just overly protective.

He was about to answer when Ally caught his eye. The wink she gave him was so subtle it was amazing. The thought struck him; *Ally was probably a pro at this. She had been dealing with Blart's condition for years.* He relaxed a little. *What am I worried about?* "No thanks, Mom. I'm going outside with Dad." He had to trust Ally could control the conversation. It was a long one too. They were in there for almost an hour. Teddy thought they were never coming out.

When they finally emerged they were laughing and chatting away. Ally must have spun some kind of magic controlling the conversation. He really wished he knew what they had been talking about. His mom either didn't dig much or couldn't get what he thought she was after. If she did, Teddy was quite sure her reaction would be completely different, so he shrugged it off. He was truly thankful their conversation lasted so long. If she had witnessed the events of the games, the questions would be endless.

Blart managed to get tied-up in the bolos and it took some time to get free. All the while, Teddy's dad was saying Blart would make a good escape artist with a little training. If that wasn't enough, Blart got tangled in the badminton net too. His accident-proneness was kicking in overtime. The lawn darts... let's just say danger; that was the quickest game played.

One toss and it was clear they didn't need to press their luck with that one. No matter what they played, Teddy's dad was oblivious to the obvious uncoordinated aspects of Blart. When the horseshoes ended up in Blart's back yard, on the roof, or even hanging on the fence, Teddy's dad would yell, "Wow, what an arm!"

Sarah heckled Teddy the whole time, which threw off his gaming skills. His throws were slightly better than Blart's, but he never got any "wows" with his performance. He was still extremely confused about what his dad saw in Blart, but regardless of the obvious challenges, they still had fun. The only game they didn't play was table pong. They didn't want to press Blart's luck with the net; and besides, Patches ran off with the balls anyway.

As the afternoon slipped into evening, they wrapped up the get-together and said their goodbyes. Teddy managed to make it through a day with Blart and maintained through all the chaos. He couldn't believe it. His parents had overlooked Blart's condition without questions. *School will be a breeze,* Teddy thought.

Chapter 20

The evening was slow and lazy, but there was a nervous feeling building inside of Teddy. It was the last night before school started and his feelings were setting in. Summer was over. Tomorrow, fourth grade would begin with a new class, new desk, new teacher, and new zombie student. Teddy couldn't help but think how Blart might be feeling. *His nerves must be running rampant.* Teddy sighed, *if Blart feels anything like I do, there probably aren't enough bones in the universe to help.*

The worst part was Teddy never got to help Blart with his biting problem. The cookout was fun, and Blart's nerves faded fast. There really wasn't any testing to do. It occurred to Teddy afterward that to properly test anything, Blart had to be exposed to uncomfortable situations. That didn't happen this time. The point of having a cookout was to enjoy people's company and make them feel comfortable. It seemed to Teddy his parents might be pros at making people feel comfortable. Who knew?

Teddy started pacing the living room, thinking hard on how to help his friend. He figured he should put his nervous energy toward something, and helping others seemed like good karma. Caught up in his own thoughts and mumbling to himself, he hadn't noticed his pacing had turned into wandering aimlessly through the house. What was he looking for? There was a nagging feeling he was close to finding it, but in truth, he was more lost than ever.

He would never get a chance to test more theories. They'd run out of time. Any kind of additional testing would have to happen at school, and that could turn disastrous. He needed a fix, and he needed one now. Wandering through the house brainstorming, he stopped in the middle of his parents' doorway.

"Are you OK, Teddy?"

His mom's voice snapped him out of it. "Huh?" he responded, confused a little. *How did I end up here?*

"You've been in the doorway mumbling something about biting and chewing to yourself. Are you OK?" his mom asked again.

Teddy sat down on the bed and looked at his mom with a big sigh. He really needed help but didn't know how to ask without giving too much away about Blart's condition. He was at a loss when his mom broke the silence.

"Teddy," she said, with her most compassionate voice. "I have a feeling you might need a little help with a sensitive problem but are afraid to ask."

Uh-oh! How much had I mumbled in the doorway, and how much had she really heard? He had to tread real lightly. "Umm, Blart and I were talking. He's been trying to train Patches," he started. How was he ever going to get this across without her radar/sonar kicking in? He trudged on, "Well, you see, Patches has been known to have a biting problem."

"Patches is a very odd dog, that's for sure," his mom replied. "Is he safe? Should I be worried?" she added quickly.

"No, Mom. It's nothing like that." He got the sudden feeling this might be headed in the wrong direction. He had to straighten it out quick, before she got suspicious. The look in her eye was already starting to change. He could see it.

"Patches likes to chew on things, not bite people. The problem is…" Teddy started again. *What was the problem?* He needed a rapid answer and was failing miserably. How could he correlate Blart's condition to Patches? He didn't know, but something nagged him to continue anyway, so he forged on. "Even though Patches has bones, he hides them and ends up chewing on other things. Blart said he started getting back into old habits again after the move."

How was any of this going to help? Patches' problem was nowhere near the same type of problem. Blart couldn't have bones in class. It wasn't like he was losing them; he just wasn't allowed to have them. It was a useless statement, he knew it, but at least it was a quick response. He still had to throw his mom off his trail. There was no telling what he said during the "mumbling episode" he had in her doorway a minute ago.

"Sounds like you might need to put Patches' bone on a chain, so he can't hide it," his mom replied. She reached behind her head trying to undo her necklace. She kept fumbling with the clasp to no avail.

"Yeah, I guess you're right. That would probably help," Teddy responded. It was no help at all really, but what could Teddy expect if he couldn't even ask the right question? He was at a loss on this one. He pondered the problem a little more as he continued to watch his mom fumble with the clasp. She had no success. There seemed to be no prospect of necklace removal in her near future if she didn't get help soon, so Teddy offered.

"Thanks," his mom said. "I can't figure out what I'm doing wrong with the clasp. It was fine when I put it on earlier today." Teddy looked closely at the clasp to see what was wrong.

There was still this nagging feeling in the back of his head he couldn't shake. He wandered in here for some reason. Why? He really had no idea but figured he might as well try and get help while he was here; he knew that. It was impossible to get help without asking a direct question, and there was no way to phrase it without breaking certain promises. He found himself in a sticky situation. *Oh well, better to leave it at that than to raise any more suspicion.*

Teddy let it go and focused back to the task at hand. He looked closely at the necklace and noticed the ring that the clasp is supposed to attach with was not in the loop at all. Instead, the clasp was hooked to the next link, which made it bind. After a few seconds, Teddy managed to manipulate it free. He pulled the necklace off and held it outstretched in his hand.

"Thank you. That was about to drive me crazy." His mom retrieved the necklace and set it into her jewelry box.

The idea struck Teddy completely out of the blue. Something hit him as he watched his mom put away the necklace. *Of course! That's it! Why hadn't I thought of that before?* "Thanks, Mom!" Teddy said, full of excitement. "You helped a bunch!" He jumped up in such a rush he bumped into the vanity, making a few bottles of perfume fall over in his haste.

"Whoa, young man. Take it slow." His mom said, as she stood the perfumes upright again.

"Sorry, Mom," Teddy responded. He crossed the room as fast as possible, trying his best not to raise suspicion. "I've got to get Blart on the phone before bed. I think you might have solved his problem."

"You mean Patches' problem, don't you?" his mom asked, raising an eyebrow. He had to get out of there, fast.

"Uh, yeah, Patches' problem. That's what I meant." Teddy looked at his mom oddly as he left. *What did she really know?* He wondered, but he didn't have time to ponder it. In fact, he had a very short amount of time. He still needed to gather supplies and get them to his bedroom. Teddy was thinking if he didn't finish before bedtime, he would at least have the supplies he needed in his room. He could work quietly all night, if he had to, with no one being the wiser. Quickening his pace, he ran as fast as possible toward the kitchen trashcan.

Chapter 21

Teddy needed a workspace; so he cleared some of the clutter on his desk, cluttering his floor in the process. It was a sacrifice that had to be made. Now wasn't the time to focus on the mess, it was time to get the last thing he needed ready for school tomorrow. Time was slipping away fast. He couldn't believe the answer was that simple, but he knew it would work. He looked at the clock. *8:37.* Putting everything he could muster into speed, he set to work.

Perspiration started to gather on his forehead, and he could feel the beads of sweat starting to move toward his eyes. He knew his tongue was halfway out of his mouth and cocked toward the corner of his upper lip. He often did that when he concentrated, and this wasn't easy work. He hammered, sawed, drilled, cut, and hammered again. It was definitely not going as fast as he wanted, and like most projects, it seemed it was going to take longer than he expected.

"What on earth is going on in here?" He heard his dad's voice ring out.

Teddy turned in enough time to see a shadow move along the wall of the hallway. His dad was close, only about two steps away. He could tell by the angle of the shadow. There was no time to hide what he was doing, and he almost went into a panic. One second later, his dad's head popped around the corner.

"What did you do to your room?" his dad asked. "It's

the night before school. If you wanted to work, I could have used you after the cookout." He crossed the room toward Teddy's desk and looked at the supplies. "What are you making anyway?"

Teddy couldn't hide what was displayed upon his desk, but if he knew his dad, it really wouldn't matter anyway. Teddy just needed to think of something plausible. "Making a model. It's a sculpture. I just needed something strong as a base." He looked back at his dad to see if he bought it.

His dad scrutinized the items on the desk, picking up the hammer and then the saw. He didn't touch the rest of the items but looked at them thoroughly. Teddy knew it looked extremely strange, but his dad surprised him. "Interesting choice of materials, son." He shook his head a little. "Looks to me like you might get a little further if you used a dremel tool. I'll get it for you. I just hope you clean up before your mom sees the mess you've created." Teddy was shocked he didn't ask any more questions.

His dad was right, of course. That dremel tool made what Teddy was trying to accomplish fast work. When he finally finished, Teddy sat back to inspect his creation. It looked right. He was sure he had made it large enough to not only last, but set right as well. While in the middle of the creative process, he got an ingenious idea; he decided to make a change. He improved the creation so that parts could be taken off when worn down and new ones could be attached. It was perfect.

The clock said 9:47. *Oh no, just a few minutes left.* He hoped it wasn't too late to phone Blart. Teddy was not the best with timing, and his mom was always quick to point it out. Had he thought about it, he would've called Blart earlier, but when the idea struck, he got caught up in the project. Pulling on the bell string and raising the can to his ear, he hoped he wasn't too late.

"Hellloo?" Blart's voice came through loud and clear.

"Hey, Blart. It's me, Teddy." He said, not thinking that it was a private line and it couldn't be anyone else. "I did it. I have the solution," he went on. "I can't really explain it right now, but I'm 100 percent confident it will work. I'll tell you about it first thing in the morning. I got to go right now. I got to clean up in a hurry or there might not be a tomorrow morning for me; especially if my mom sees the mess I just made."

"OK, seee you innn the morrrning," the response came.

Teddy cleaned up as fast as he could, threw on his pajamas, and headed downstairs for the family tradition. Sunday nights they watched "Tall Tales of the Weird and Strange" together.

It was one of those science-fiction mind-bending shows where weird things would happen to everyday people. The effects could be anything from waking in an altered dimension to growing scaly skin. The afflicted always believed they were going crazy. Strange and bizarre things would happen around them, which would drive them crazier throughout the program. It was one of those shows that was completely outlandish but made you think afterward. He liked that. Teddy loved their Sunday night tradition.

The clock said 9:59 as he flopped down on the couch between his mom and dad, his usual place for the viewing. He made it just in time. His dad raised an eyebrow and Teddy nodded, completing the silent exchange. It was his dad's way of asking, "Did you clean up your mess?" Teddy and his dad communicated like that a lot. More than anyone noticed. It was sly, and Teddy liked that. It was like they had a secret unspoken language.

The program started and Teddy laid back, putting his feet on the ottoman. It was about a kid that had an accident and suddenly became clairvoyant. The kid could touch things and tell you not only where the object had been, but what it had been used for. When he touched something of his own, he could see his future. The twist was he could only see up until the item was no longer his. He kept holding things in his room but only saw part of his future. He would try to trace his life forward, attempting to find items in his visions he didn't have yet.

Teddy started thinking about what it might be like to know the future. *Would you be able to change it? Would it take the excitement away from new things? Could you use it like time travel to know future events, then help the world avoid pitfalls to humanity?* The ideas were endless. That's exactly what Teddy loved about the show. It got your mind started. Sometimes it rode the edge though, and it could almost scare you.

One episode was about a portal under a bed. It would open after one went to sleep in a certain hotel room. People would have to pull over on a deserted highway due to obscure events. Things like a washed out bridge, a random sandstorm on the horizon, or a rockslide that blocks the road. Right on cue, a random stranger always showed up. He'd explain the road was impassable, or too dangerous. Next, he would mention a hotel close by; one they could stay at until the road was cleared or the hazard had passed. Sure enough, the hotel would be under remodel, they would get the only room available, and somehow they'd disappear without a trace by morning. *Yeah, try and go to sleep after that one.*

Teddy remembered one time curling up in a state of

panic, trying his hardest not to go to sleep. When he woke up that morning, he twisted his ankle jumping from his bed. He had to jump as far as he could, so he wouldn't get sucked into any portals. It didn't dawn on him he had fallen asleep during the night, and there wasn't any portal, since he hadn't disappeared.

Teddy drifted off into thought, not paying attention to the episode. He started thinking about the last two days and how his life could be an episode of its own. The things that had happened were outlandish by any definition, and Teddy knew the tale was probably just beginning. He smiled, thinking about his life as an episode of "Tall Tale of the Weird and Strange" was funny. He couldn't help but let his grin get wider reflecting on how the last few days would make a great episode.

Teddy hadn't noticed the show had ended. He was deep in his own thoughts about his solution for Blart. Time slipped by fast, but Teddy didn't mind. He wasn't under pressure anymore. In fact, he was very relaxed. He only had to brush his teeth and double-check his backpack before bed. Then it would be morning, and he would be on his way with Blart to start the fourth grade.

He finished his bathroom routine and paused by the hook in the hall. Teddy unzipped the front pocket of the backpack, and double-checked to make sure he had everything packed. Not only had he slipped the solution for Blart's chewing habit inside before the Sunday night tradition started, he had also slipped in the most important thing you could have if you were friends with Blart. Liquid bandage!

It was still there, along with a small spool of fishing line, some clips and ties for the quick fix, and a couple of rolls of tape. He hoped he had everything he needed in what he fashioned as a Blart medical kit. *When your best friend is a zombie, you have to be prepared.*

Looking at the items he had gathered, he figured his dad would be proud of his planning and preparation. He really thought this one through. Everything seemed to be in order. The medical supplies were all packed up in a small box, but now that Teddy was looking at it, he realized it needed one more thing. Taking out the new markers he needed for class, Teddy opened the pack and quickly found the red. He set the small box on the floor and drew a straight line down and one straight across. Finding the black, he drew a circle around the cross in the center. He looked at the medical symbol he had drawn on the box and knew it was complete. Slipping the markers and medical kit back inside, Teddy zipped the backpack shut. He was ready for tomorrow! Heading to his room, Teddy turned off his light and slipped into bed.

Chapter 22

The morning came suddenly, and with it, the excitement of fourth grade. You weren't the top of the school yet, that was reserved for the fifth-graders, but you were close. That gave you clout and swagger among the younger grades. It really meant more opportunities opening up at recess. There was a pecking order of territories; the older you were the more you could do more on the playground.

That wasn't the excitement Teddy felt though. He was excited about the solution he thought of for Blart and was starting to feel impatient. Teddy wanted to run outside and give it to him right away. Unfortunately, he still had to get dressed, eat breakfast and triple check his packing; he needed to make sure his medical kit was still there. Hopefully his mom didn't forget something and open the backpack again. She was bound to see it, and that might raise a ton of questions he was not prepared to answer.

Teddy had to hurry and get to the table fast, so he could keep his eyes on his mom's movements, just in case. Running to the bathroom, he finished in lightning time. If getting ready was an Olympic sport, Teddy was sure he would've medaled in the event. He rushed to the kitchen in time to see his mom cooking and his dad setting the table.

"Are you a little nervous about the fourth grade, Teddy?" she asked as he sat down.

"No, Mom. Why?" He grabbed for a hot waffle.

"No reason. Is it a new trend to wear your shirt backwards with two different socks?"

Teddy looked down at his shirt. *Oops.* Well, the Olympic judges would have to deduct points for the shirt, but he figured the socks should earn him style points. Plus, he'd never been through a true getting ready competition and didn't know if speed and accuracy were the only judged categories. He was a little embarrassed, and in a true competition probably would've been knocked from the podium, with no chance to medal. If you asked him though, his speed still showed promise.

Turning his shirt around, Teddy started into his breakfast with urgency. He kept looking out the window to see if Blart was ready, but he hadn't emerged from his house yet. When he realized he hadn't even begun to think about what Blart must be feeling, Teddy got a guilty feeling inside; his new friend's nerves could be running rampant. If he was in Blart's shoes, his teeth might sound like someone using a jackhammer inside the house. Straining to listen, all he heard was the sound of forks on plates around him. He hoped his friend was all right. If he didn't see him come out soon, he'd just have to go over and investigate. Teddy finished as fast as he could, trying to give himself a little extra time. The solution was in his backpack, and Blart could be in nervous knots right now. If Blart had what Teddy made for him... well, it could only help.

Finishing his breakfast then washing his dishes, Teddy worked as fast as he could. He grabbed the backpack off the hook in the hall, only unzipping it enough to spot the items he was most concerned about. They were still there and untouched; that was good. It meant two things; his mom was thorough in her original packing, making sure he was armed with the supplies needed to march down the road of knowledge. More importantly though, it meant she hadn't reopened the bag. Feeling relieved, Teddy headed toward the door where his mom waited to see him off, holding his lunch.

He grabbed the "Mega Robot Morpher" lunch pail from her hand as she kissed him goodbye. They had picked it out together for this year. It was the coolest, because it came with a morphing robot thermos. In fact, Teddy's mom had to order it special delivery, so he knew other kids wouldn't be carrying the same one. Most kids would stick with the "Action Hero Crime Fighters" this year. That was respectable, but Teddy liked cutting edge, and nothing stated cutting edge better than a morphing robot thermos.

Stepping outside, Teddy made a beeline straight for Blart's door. He approached hearing a strange sound that got louder as he got closer. Teddy looked around cautiously, wondering what it could be. When the door opened, the sound blasted him in the face. It sounded like a washing machine knocking around during the spin cycle mixed with the hum of a microwave.

"Mom, I'm going to be late if we don't leave soon! Can't I walk by myself? I'm seven now!"

"No," Ally responded, "Blart will be ready in a minute."

Sarah just looked at Teddy and pushed past toward the sidewalk to sit down. "I don't know why I can't go. Look at you. If they let a stupid six-year-old go by himself, they should let me go too."

"I'm nine," Teddy replied, for the hundredth time in two days. He turned back to the open door and faced the sound again. Even the abrasiveness of the sound was easier to take than a conversation with Sarah. He stepped inside and saw Ally with Blart. He was so nervous his jaw was working overtime, clicking so fast it almost sounded like loud humming. Every so often his jaw would spasm and clack together with another louder knocking sound. Teddy realized he not only found the microwave, but the spin cycle as well.

"Blart, it's OK, you can calm down," Teddy said as he moved closer.

Blart looked at Teddy, and the sound from his jaw started changing tone. It slowed a little rhythmically and started to sound like a train moving along a track. Teddy kept at it, "Don't worry, we're in the same class. I'll be with you all day, you'll see." The sound slowed again, to that of a galloping horse. It was working! Blart was just nervous, and Teddy understood. The first day of a new school could give anyone anxiety.

"He's been getting nervous all morning. I wish he would just chew a little and get it out, but for some reason he keeps trying to go without his bone." That statement would've been odd to anyone else, but this was normal for anybody who really knew Blart. "He keeps going on about no bones in the fourth grade." Ally said.

"I think I might have had something to do with that." Teddy responded, his shoulders sinking slightly. He knew he had everything to do with that but didn't know it would affect Blart so much. "Hey, Blart. Remember when I said I found a solution?" Teddy continued. The galloping sound changed from one horse to two as he nodded his head, making his jaw shake in a funny way. "Well here it is," Teddy said, reaching into his backpack.

His hand came out slowly, and with it was a small wire with items attached. Teddy handed it to Blart so he could take a closer peek. As he looked at Teddy's solution, his jaw slowed and soon stopped. He couldn't believe it. He never expected

anyone outside of his family to be so accepting of him. Teddy was the ultimate friend, and he proved it over and over. There in Blart's hand was a necklace. Unlike ordinary necklaces, in-between the looped wires were small bones. They'd been filed down to look like stones, but there was no mistake, they were made of bone.

Ally looked at the exchange and her heart almost burst. No matter what happened with them, the two boys would face it together, as best friends, she knew. She reached down and took the necklace from Blart. Placing it around his neck, she fastened the clasp. It was a perfect fit. It was tight enough not to hang too low but long enough to get the bones in his mouth. He bit down and flashed a wonky grin at Teddy.

Ally watched the pair gather their stuff and retrieve Sarah from the sidewalk. They looked like they were made to be together. Best friends forever; not to be cliché. Teddy looked at Ally once more. "Don't worry, I packed liquid bandage." He tapped the backpack as he spoke. Turning around and walking down the road, the pair headed toward school with Sarah in tow. Ally smiled to herself. She knew their adventures were just starting as she watched them walk away.

If you like this book series please
sign-up for our email list @
whatkindanameisblart.com/subscribe.
We offer occasional prize give-aways and
more to our loyal subscribers.

Please leave a "brief" review
for Chewing Problems on
Amazon.com

Your support makes it possible
for our author to bring you
more great books.
Thank you!

Follow us on

Meet the Author
Dominic Cosmé

A child at heart, Dominic Cosme has found a special enjoyment for writing children's literature. "When I think on my life, it makes sense to find enjoyment in this medium. I have always loved the creative process, and I have truly found my voice in writing." He was first published by Sparrowgrass Poetry Forum in 1991, Poetic Voices of America. In addition to writing, Dominic has always had a passion for reading. He started reading early and has been an avid reader since. His reading interests span from the classics, to Science Fiction, Historical Novels, and even some Young Adult; he loves them all.

With a background in composition, Dominic plays several instruments. "Playing instruments can strengthen the brain more than any other activity. With my history in music, it makes sense that writing comes so naturally to me". He finds playing music to be helpful in relaxing and focusing his thoughts, as well as having many other benefits that contribute to a healthy mind and body.

Living in Denton, Texas, with his wife and three children (all boys, two of which are twins!), he's never short on inspiration.

He spends time skatboarding, playing soccer, and gaming, with his kids. Staying active with his children and in-touch with the youth remains important to him.

Like other artists and authors, Dominic depends on his loyal audience to support him by following his books online. Thank you for your support!

CPSIA information can be obtained
at www.ICGtesting.com
Printed in the USA
FSOW02n1046281017
40310FS

9 780999 236109